I0775480

Honeymoon for Six

CHRIS KENISTON

Indie House Publishing

Indie House Publishing

MORE BOOKS
By Chris Keniston

The Billionaire Barons of Texas
Just One Date
Just One Spark
Just One Dance
Just One Take
Just One Taste
Just One Shot
Just One Chance

Hart Land
Heather
Lily
Violet
Iris
Hyacinth
Rose
Calytrix
Zinnia
Poppy
Picture Perfect

Farraday Country
Adam
Brooks
Connor
Declan
Ethan
Finn
Grace
Hannah
Ian
Jamison

Keeping Eileen
Loving Chloe
Morgan
Neil
Owen

Honeymoon Series

Honeymoon for One
Honeymoon for Three
Honeymoon for Four
Honeymoon for Five
Honeymoon for Six

Aloha Romance Series:

Aloha Texas
Almost Paradise
Mai Tai Marriage
Dive Into You
Look of Love
Love by Design
Love Walks In
Shell Game
Flirting with Paradise

Surf's Up Flirts:

(Aloha Series Companions)
Shall We Dance
Love on Tap
Head Over Heels
Perfect Match
Just One Kiss
It Had to Be You
Cat's Meow

ACKNOWLEDGMENTS

I can't remember which authors were in my living room when we came up with the idea of a reality game show, but thank you anyhow!

Despite recovering from covid, hanging out with my grandchildren, and flying across the ocean, I actually had a lot of fun writing Jo and Dylan's story. Though, it's the across the ocean part that matters for this book. I have to thank my dear friend author Olivia Sands for opening her home and then prodding me with a back scratcher every time I got distracted from my daily word count. You're the best! And a great cook too!

Most of all, thank you guys for sticking with us through five cruises!

CHAPTER ONE

"**F**or the love of all that is holy, please leave that turn of the last century getup in the closet!" Josephine Ummarino, known to her closest friends as Jo, and to her oversized Italian family as Giuseppa, shook her head at her eldest sister. "What kind of a woman wears something like that to her one and only bachelorette party?"

"The kind who wishes you'd stop treating this trip like a strip club training program and more like the fun girls trip it's supposed to be. I mean, weren't you the one who told Angie how much you loved the idea of an ordinary last-night party instead of a bachelorette party?" Mina, the soon-to-be bride, shot her youngest sister a piercing glare.

"I did, but this is different." Jo shrugged. The whole idea of a few close family and friends going off on a ten-day cruise was in itself *different*. Most traditional bachelorette parties were a long weekend at best, but Mina wanted this to be more of a special time with the women closest to her, so a long cruise won.

Shaking her head, Mina rolled her eyes and blew out a frustrated sigh.

"I still don't understand why you couldn't do your party at Uncle Vinny's pizzeria." Jo's mom stirred the gravy she'd been simmering on her daughter's stove for hours. "He has a really nice room in the back."

"Mama." Jo tried really hard not to whine, but they'd explained to their mother more than once that a dark room in the back of their uncle's aging pizza parlor was not the send-off to married life that she and Ginnie, the middle sister, had planned for Mina. "You can't compare Uncle

Vinny's restaurant to ten days on the azure-blue Caribbean."

"You want blue?" Her mother waved a spoon at her. "Uncle Vinny can paint the walls." Antoinette Ummarino turned back to her simmering sauce. "Blue is a nice color."

Mina shook her head at Jo, signaling it was time to change the subject.

Knowing her sister was right, Jo leaned into her mom and kissed her on the cheek. "We can have a nice rehearsal dinner at Uncle Vinny's. How does that sound?"

Her mother shrugged, but Jo could tell the woman was hiding a smile. "I'll let him know." A lazy grin erupted. "Maybe we'll still paint the room blue."

Jo and the other sisters chuckled. "Blue is a nice color."

"What about this?" Ginnie held a floral sundress up to her chin. "Too much color?"

"No such thing as too much color," their mother muttered.

"I like it." Mina nodded. "With your figure, that dress will have heads turning."

"Who knows," Jo flashed a toothy grin, "maybe you'll find a man of your own."

"That's all I need, find a nice guy on board who lives somewhere across the country. No thanks." Ginnie shook her head, and set the dress aside. "Maybe I'll stick to cotton shirts and capris."

"Chicken," Jo squawked.

Ginnie smiled widely. "If the feather fits, wear it."

"Oh, brother." Mina rolled her eyes. "If there's ever an award for the worst clichés, Ginnie, you'd win every time."

Her sister shrugged. "Like I said, if the feather fits…"

The three fell into fits of giggles the way they'd done since they were little kids. Jo couldn't believe Mina would be getting married and moving out of the house they'd shared the last few years. A lot of sisters didn't get along, but she couldn't imagine her world without Ginnie and Mina in it. Truth be told, she was probably looking forward to this cruise more than her sister. Not that she wasn't happy with her life, but some days, staring at a computer all day and then watching television with your sisters at night just felt, well, geriatric. Everyone should have a little adventure in their life once in a while, and she was more than ready to add a little excitement to hers. This was one last chance for some serious sister/girl fun. To live it up, at least for the next ten days.

"Where's the love of my life?" The voice of Mina's soon-to-be husband, Kent, whom she'd met on the one and only cruise the sisters had ever taken, carried through the large home.

Another thing Jo loved was the way her sister lit up at anything to do with Kent. Jo could only hope that some day she too would meet that special someone who makes her feel like she sat on top of the world—just not yet. She still had a lot of fun things she wanted to do before settling down to home and hearth.

Giving his soon-to-be bride a kiss that was just hot enough to warm the room a degree or two, but sweet enough to make their mother smile, Kent stepped back and enveloped Mina's hand in his. "Everyone all packed?"

"Almost!" Ginnie grabbed the colorful dress she'd debated and headed down the hall and up the stairs.

"I'm ready." Jo had been packed for more than a week but she wasn't going to share that little tidbit of information.

"Me too. Though," Mina grinned up at Kent, a mischievous twinkle in her eyes, "I could probably leave some room if you want to stowaway."

He kissed her temple and lowered his voice. "You have no idea how much I wish I could."

"Oh, I might." With those few words and their gazes steady and locked on each other, the temperature in the room inched higher again.

Blowing out a low sigh, Jo had always thought her life was full and fun, but suddenly she felt like something was truly missing. Not that this cruise would change that. After all, the odds of a major computer fiasco booking total strangers in the same room happening a second time were beyond slim to none. Too bad, right about now being confined in a cabin with an available hunk didn't feel like such a bad idea at all.

Dylan Barnes had several good things in his life, a mother who was a walking poster child for unconditional maternal love, even if she had a dictatorial streak during his childhood, a father who supported his every effort whether sound or foolish, a sister who let him think he was smarter than her even though they both knew it wasn't true, and a best friend who had been more like a brother since they were born three months apart to their sorority sister mothers. Mothers who also happened to be next-door neighbors for most of the boys' lives. The best friend was his current dilemma. For a lot of people, having a close friend in show business was beyond intriguing. Even if that friend worked behind the scenes and not in front of the camera. Carson Bennett had finally been made associate producer of a reality television game show, *Love on Deck.*

Now, Dylan's long-planned trip with his best friend would be doubling as a working vacation for Carson. Which meant that Dylan would be spending the next ten nights on a floating hotel for the production of the new show. Personally, Dylan found these dating/find-the-love-of-your-life television shows absurd, but he did indeed want to help cheer his friend on. He just wished he could do it another time from his living room recliner. And so did Dylan's associates. Even though he had weeks of unused vacation time and sick leave coming to him, the timing for taking two weeks of it couldn't have been worse. When they'd originally planned their trip, neither had any idea that Carson would be getting his own show or that the biggest client the family firm had ever courted would be on the lookout for a new law firm. On top of that, being short one attorney wasn't helping. Especially since as of Monday morning, his dad and he were dead smack in the middle of the most crucial negotiations the firm had ever participated in. The boost to the company's bottom line and reputation was almost immeasurable.

Of course if his last name wasn't Barnes, and if his

mother wasn't so excited for her best friend's son, this trip would not be happening at all. Being a junior partner in Barnes & Barnes Attorneys at Law had its pros and cons. The first attorney in the family had been Jedediah Barnes. When his son joined the firm it had become Barnes & Barnes. For over a hundred years there had always been at least two generations of Barnes at the firm. Until a few years ago there had been three. He still missed his grandfather's silent strength.

"You do realize that most adult men would kill for a chance to take a luxury cruise filled with bikini-clad young women and have VIP access to the filming of a soon-to-be hit television show." Carson rolled his eyes. "From the look on your face anyone would think instead of giving you a dream opportunity, I was asking you to walk the plank."

"Sorry. Long day at work."

"You have a lot of those lately. You should just tell your dad that you gave the firm your best effort but it's not for you. You need to do what makes you really happy."

Carson made at least some sense. More than once in the last few months Dylan had wondered just how awful would it be to take the leap and walk away from the law and turn his wood working hobby into a new career. Until he'd look at his notice of rental increase along with his bills and other expenses, then imagine breaking his father's heart, and he'd put the dream of working with his hands off for another day. Or year.

"What you should have done was tried out for the show. A quarter of a million dollars grand prize would go a long way to funding that furniture business you're always talking about."

Shaking his head, Dylan sighed. "First of all, these crazy competition reality shows are, well, crazy. Second, unless you carry around a magic hat that I could pull the perfect partner out of, auditioning for the show wasn't an option." He knew full well that excuse would go over more easily with Carson than the argument that he thought the whole premise was dumb.

"First of all," Carson waved a hand at him, "no one

knows for sure if anyone is the perfect partner. Remember, none of the contestants have actually met in person yet. They've only known each other online. Now the show will be the test of true love. And second, what about Colleen?"

"What about her?"

"You two are close. I'm sure she would have done the show with you."

"We're friends, not soul mates. Besides, we've already met in person. No surprises there."

Carson shrugged. "Don't let the word reality fool you."

"All the more reason to watch a good movie on TV instead."

The words were barely past Dylan's lips when his friend's phone blared the theme from the old television show *Love Boat.* It took everything in Dylan not to roll his eyes, or worse, gag. Carson frowned, grunted, bobbed his head a time or two, then sighed. Whatever was going down, from the pained expression on his best friend's face, it wasn't anything good.

His brows buckled with concern, Carson turned, and still listening to the voice on the other end of the phone, leveled his gaze with Dylan's. Carson stared at him and very slowly a lazy grin tipped up at one end of his mouth then the other. "No worries. I've got this." A few more grunts and nods and Carson disconnected the call and slid his phone into his pocket.

"Problems?"

"Depends."

"On?"

"What's Colleen doing for the next two weeks?" Carson stood, arms crossed, grinning like the proverbial cat who'd eaten the canary.

"I don't know, and something tells me I don't want to know."

"There are three couples on this first season."

"Season? You've only got a ten-day cruise."

Carson shrugged. "We have fifteen episodes planned. With ten days of footage that should not be a problem. Viewers will be voting on taped—and obviously edited—episodes."

"How can you air who's in the lead each episode if the viewers haven't voted yet?" The words were barely out of Dylan's mouth when he held up his hand. "Never mind. Forget I asked. I really don't need or want to know."

"Good, because right now none of it is important. One of the final couples was in a car accident. The girlfriend had to go into surgery. She'll have to do rehab next so there's no way they can do the show."

"I don't like the way you're looking at me."

To Dylan's chagrin, Carson's smile grew wider. "Call Colleen. Tell her you guys are going on an all expenses paid cruise, and a chance to win two hundred and fifty thousand dollars."

"But we're not in love." From what he understood, the whole premise of the show was for the couple still madly in love after ten days of making nice in person *and* scoring the most points on random daily challenges would win the big bucks.

"Details. Remember, don't let the word reality fool you."

"I am not going to play games with Colleen for the sake of your show. Don't you have backup couples?"

"No, we don't have backup couples available on two days notice, this is a new show. Listen, the first run of a new antique appraisal show, the crew had to pull people in from off the street. In some ways, I'm doing the same thing. If you tell Colleen up front what this is all about, you won't be playing games—you'll be playing for a lot of money. Maybe you should just ask her?"

That gave him pause. He supposed if both he and Colleen knew this was all for show—and prize money— maybe it wouldn't be so bad. The least he should probably do was ask her. After all, one hundred and twenty-five thousand dollars would give him plenty of breathing room to turn his hobby into a profitable business. "I'll call her, but if she says no, you'll have to find your show another patsy."

It took all of thirty seconds to call Colleen and another fifteen seconds to explain the situation and only a short instant for her to screech in his ear. "I'll never have to buy another lottery ticket again!"

One brief illogical sentence and Dylan knew he was about to become a contestant on a television game show. Heaven help them all.

CHAPTER TWO

er nose to the air like a blood hound picking up the scent of a missing person, Jo took in a deep breath and smiled. "I really do love the smell of the ocean."

Standing to one side, her older sister Mina smiled, shaking her head. "This is not the ocean. This is a Florida port and it smells more like oil tankers than the ocean, but give us a few hours and I'll be right there with you. I really do love cruising."

"Back at ya," Ginnie agreed, bobbing her head.

"There you are." Angela, their next-door neighbor and the person who originally convinced them cruising is fun, came to their side. "When you text someone that you're on the upper deck with other passengers, you might want to get a tad more specific. I've walked all around this deck before I spotted Ginnie. Great dress, by the way."

"Thank you." Ginnie grinned proudly and spun in place. "I was worried it might be too colorful, but apparently color has a valuable purpose."

Mina pulled out her phone and tapped a message.

"Don't tell me you're texting your fiancé already." Jo rolled her eyes. "We're not even out of port yet."

"Troublemaker. I'm texting Teresa. Letting her know we're on the upper deck overlooking the pool, pretty much dead center."

"Oh, for the love of Mom's lasagna, don't use the word dead while we're all standing on a massive heap of metal that has no business staying afloat." Ginnie took a step back from the rail.

"Don't start getting Nervous Nellie on me. The boat is

perfectly safe."

"That's what they said about the Titanic." Ginnie flashed a cheesy grin. "I know we're going to have a great time, just avoid tragic adjectives until we dock in ten days."

"Got it." Mina flashed a toothy grin. "I won't say a word about Poseidon."

Shaking her head, Ginnie lightly smacked her sister on the arm. "Just you wait, Henry Higgins."

"Yoo hoo." Teresa, a typical Italian beauty with curves to match, waved at them as she made her way across the deck. "Isn't this where we meet good-looking men?"

"That's right." Angela bobbed her head at her neighbor's cousin. "This is where you mentioned having first met the men on the last cruise."

"Not just any men, the love of Mina's life," Jo added.

Ginnie, ever the practical sister, rolled her eyes. "Like that's going to happen twice in a lifetime."

"Oh look," Teresa pointed behind Mina, "drinks with those pretty little umbrellas."

Behind the group of women, a waiter walked past the passengers with a tray of frozen orange colored drinks topped with a colorful little paper umbrella.

"Do you suppose they're free?" Jo asked.

Teresa shrugged. "Looks like it."

The waiter moved slowly toward them, handing out a drink or two before reaching them.

"Do you need our cabin number?" Ginnie asked.

"No, ma'am. These are courtesy bon voyage cocktails."

"Works for me." Jo grabbed a glass from the tray and the others followed suit.

Phone in one hand, and drink in the other, Mina stared down at her screen, squinted, then looked up scanning the deck.

"Something wrong?" Ginnie asked.

Mina shook her head. "Brenda just texted that she's on board and looking for us."

"Next cruise I'm bringing a sign like those chauffeurs at the airports hold up. This way we can all find each other more quickly." Jo was only partially teasing. Brenda was

Mina's best friend since college and soon to be maid of honor. She also was lighting up Mina's phone with texts. Apparently upper deck, dead center, was not easy to find. If not a sign, maybe a huge colorful hat that could be spotted a mile away.

The five women raised their glasses in a toast at the moment that Brenda came scurrying past the passengers leaning along the railing enjoying the ambiance.

"This is so seriously cool." Brenda's gaze darted from one fruity drink to another. "Any more where those came from?"

Mina raised her hand and waved down a different crew member with a full tray of drinks.

"So what's on the agenda for today?" Looking at the ladies over the rim of her drink, Brenda took a sip.

"As little as possible." Ginnie grinned. "We have dinner at 6:30 and then I plan to just scope out the ship and start decompressing."

Jo couldn't blame her sister, the demands of her job had her functioning on her last nerve. "I saw a few signs posted for a new TV show filming on board."

"Really?" Teresa spun around. "Which one?"

"Don't know, but I bet it will be fun."

Teresa's back snapped straight and a knowing grin took over her face. "Drool-worthy at nine o'clock."

Five heads snapped in that direction.

"Subtlety is not you guys' forte, is it?" Teresa shook her head.

"There are thousands of people on this ship." Jo shrugged. "No way we could do anything to stand out." But she had to give her cousin credit, there was a group of guys standing across the way and from what she could see, they were all worthy of a magazine cover. She took another sip and for the first time since this trip was planned, wondered if maybe lightening could indeed strike twice?

Standing in the parking lot, staring at the massive cruise ship, Dylan's former college suite mate and best female friend ever, stared up slack jawed. "Oh, wow. This boat is as big as a city."

"Yes, it is." Dylan had to admit, with the specs on these huge ships, his mind knew they were big, but standing up close, the size was beyond impressive.

Slapping her hands together and rubbing them enthusiastically, Colleen swirled around to face him. "This is the most exciting thing I've done since my twenty-first birthday in Vegas. I can hardly wait."

"Then let's get this show on the road." Smiling, Dylan handed a tip to the porters at the dock, prayed that their luggage actually made it to their cabins, and extended his elbow to his game show partner.

They'd barely wound their way through the port terminal when his phone blew up with a string of texts. All from Carson.

"Something wrong?" Colleen glanced over his arm at the phone.

"It seems the show is starting earlier than I expected. Film crew is onboard and waiting to get footage of us when the ship pulls out."

Colleen glanced down at her watch. "But that's not for two hours."

Shrugging one shoulder, he waved a hand in the air. "I'm just delivering the message."

"Then I guess the show's starting sooner than later." Colleen leaned into his shoulder when the ship's photographer snapped their photo at the top of the escalator, and then it dawned on Dylan that they had a part to play for this show, and the prize money. Letting his arm slip down, he grabbed hold of her hand, and lifting it to place a gentle kiss on the back of her hand, he grinned at her. "Here we go. *Dear*."

Rolling her eyes, Colleen softly chuckled and barely shook her head. "If we're going to pull this off, you'd better come up with a better term of endearment than that. It sounds like a salutation to your maiden aunt."

"For the record, I have never called any aunt dear." Even if he only had one.

Still holding hands they checked in, crossed the last section of the terminal and proceeded up the gangway.

"This is so exciting." Colleen squeezed his hand and he had to admit, even if he wasn't thrilled about the entire reason for being here, he was a bit excited at the possibilities as well.

His phone buzzed. A text from his mom. *Wish we could be there with you to support Carson and his new show, but you know your father and his work. Have a good time. Love you.*

He quickly tapped a response of I love you too. He knew how badly his mother had wanted to come and support Carson, but without his dad, she thought about it briefly and passed. It was better that way. He hadn't had the opportunity—or nerve—to tell her of the change of plans and that he would be participating on the show. Not to mention, he had no idea how any of this would go over with the new client negotiations, but he doubted shenanigans on a reality show added to the firm's credibility as stellar legal advisors. His best bet was to keep the whole crazy project under the radar from his family and the potential client until the deal was signed and sealed. Hopefully, Carson's mom would be successful at keeping his mother away from the television show for a while. Though he had no idea how she'd pull that one off. Once he was home again and it was all over and done with, he could face the storm. Hopefully, a hundred and twenty-five thousand dollars richer.

Of course there was no concern about keeping his father in the dark. Dylan doubted his dad would be anywhere near a TV for some time. For Robert Barnes, courting the Costa Brewery account had become the closest thing to an obsession that Dylan could remember. Landing that account would be a nice feather in the law firm's cap, and his father wanted that more than anything he'd wanted in a very long time. So, Dylan's mom was supporting her friend's son from afar, and Dylan's dad and sister were tasked with wining and dining and winning over the owner of the largest brewery in the Americas.

Stepping off the gangway, Dylan and Colleen crossed the promenade deck in search of the glass elevators to the pool deck where all the revelers were. As the elevator inched its way up, the grin on Colleen's face slipped.

"You okay?" He was still holding her hand and felt it go a little clammy.

Without saying a word she nodded, swallowed, and then taking in a deep breath, eased into a slow but steady smile. "I think the glass elevator is giving me a touch of vertigo. I'll be fine on deck again."

"Yeah, not everyone can handle the bottom dropping out from under them, so to speak."

She closed her eyes and swallowed hard. "I wish you wouldn't say things like that."

"Sorry." He tried not to chuckle.

The elevator came to a stop and a wave of fresh air hit them both as they stepped onto the deck. He was thankful to see the earnest smile return to Colleen's face. It didn't take long to scope out the film crew. To his surprise with all the people hurrying about, the passengers were almost oblivious to the presence of the crew with lights and small movie cameras. People of all ages and sizes either staked their claim to the lounge chairs and were already soaking up the warm sun, or were leaning against the railing staring off at what would soon be a seafaring horizon.

It had been centuries since Dylan had taken a real vacation and with every passing moment, he was growing more enthused at the prospect of ten glorious days away from the demands of the family business.

"Look at that." Colleen released her hold on his hand and scurried across the swatch of deck to lean against the railing, her finger pointing across the port to a row of huge houses on the opposite shore. "Wouldn't it be fun to live in one of those?"

"Their taxes must be a killer."

"Party pooper." Colleen's left arm flung out and smacked him across the chest. Leaning heavily against the railing, he could see her grip tighten and thought she swayed back ever so slightly.

"Waiter." A pretty blonde standing with a group of women beside Colleen held up an empty glass. "Another round please."

"How many?" the waiter with an empty tray asked.

The blonde called out, "Six. Oh wait." She turned to Colleen. "Would you like a drink?"

Colleen forced a smile and barely nodded.

"Make that seven."

"Thank you." Colleen's smile seemed to fade and her grip on the rail appeared to tighten, but with all the people, Dylan couldn't easily get closer.

"I'm Jo." The blonde stuck her hand out to Colleen.

"Nice to meet you." Colleen let go of the rail, spun around, and floundered left then right. "Can we tell the captain to stop rocking the boat?"

The blonde's brows arched high. "We're not moving. Yet."

"Oh, boy." Colleen swayed again, this time bumping against the blonde.

To her credit, the woman grabbed Colleen by the arms and nudged her into a nearby chair. "No offense, but you're looking a little green. Do you get seasick?"

"Don't know. Never been on a boat before." Colleen kept one hand on her mouth and another on her stomach. "I don't think I feel very good."

Dylan finally cut through the people walking back and forth and hurried up to stand beside the blonde and Colleen. "Do you want to go to your room and lie down?"

She started to nod, and quickly decided that wasn't a good idea. "I'm not sure I want to move."

"Maybe a ginger ale?" The friendly stranger looked around. The other women in her group were consumed in conversation and didn't seem to notice that anything was amiss. "Where's a waiter when you need one?"

Just then one of the women came to stand behind the blonde. "Is something wrong?"

"I think she's seasick."

Another woman inched closer. "I have some pills in my

bag in the room, but once we sail, the stores will sell those wrist bands. Not sure about the sea-sick patches. You may need to get those from the infirmary."

The blonde turned to face Dylan and took a step closer to him. Looking up, he could see the concern in her eyes. Something he hadn't expected from a total stranger. "I don't think she should move. If you'll go see about something stronger for her, we'll keep an eye—"

"There you are." A man he didn't recognize came up beside him. "Carson is waiting for you two. Better hurry."

The blonde glanced wide-eyed at the strange man, but said nothing.

"Colleen isn't feeling well," he explained.

The man looked the blonde over from head to toe. "Looks fine to me, let's go." Without another word, he shifted behind them and nudged them forward. "No time to waste, the ship is leaving port any minute and Carson wants to have all three couples on film when the horn blows."

"You don't understand." Dylan shook his head, glancing down at Colleen to see her eyes closed and most of the color drained from her face.

"Just go," his best friend managed to mutter.

"Look." The guy gave them another gentle nudge. "Either you move it now or we're all going to be in trouble."

"Trouble?" The blonde glanced up at Dylan. "Who are you and what have you done?"

CHAPTER THREE

Visions of being whisked off to some tiny island country in the middle of nowhere and sold to the highest bidder played before Jo's eyes. Looking over her shoulder, she could see her family hovering over Colleen like mother hens, oblivious to her current dilemma. As pitiful as the timing was, the first thing to cross Jo's mind was not for someone to save her, but how proud her mom would be of her girls.

"Wait a minute." Common sense kicked into gear. She was on a huge ship and still in US waters. Digging her heels into the ground, so to speak, she managed to stutter to a halt. "What the hell is going on?"

"There you are. We've been waiting." Another gentleman came rushing up to them and stopped in front of the guy who'd been with the girl who had turned lovely shades of green. The newest guy flashed a sharp glare the man beside her and then doing a double take, looked at Jo. "Who are you?"

"That's what I want to know." She crossed her arms. It was about as much of a show of force as she could muster.

"You don't know who you are?" The new guy's brows arched high on his forehead.

"Of course I do. What I want to know is who are you?"

"Carson Bennett. Associate producer of *Love on Deck.*"

Now Jo's eyes rounded like a startled owl. "The new TV show?"

"Excuse me." The guy with the sick friend held up both his hands. "We have a problem."

All three of them, the new guy, the nudger, and Jo, snapped their heads around to face him.

"Colleen is seasick. We can't shoot a sailing away scene. You'll have to do it without us."

"Shoot?" Jo blinked. "As in filming?"

Both guys nodded, then the second one stared at Jo. "You want to win some money?"

"What?" Things were moving from weird to insane. All she could think to do was take a step back. First chance she got she'd bolt to her sisters. Maybe spend the rest of the cruise in her room. It was a nice cabin—with a window.

"Colleen is on this cruise with Dylan to win a share of two hundred and fifty thousand dollars. If you can pull it off instead, the three of you can figure out how to split it. But right now I have a show to shoot and if we don't boogie the whole thing is going to go up in smoke."

Both Jo and the man named Dylan sputtered their objections. The words *wait, but, no,* and *hang on,* stumbled over each other as the first guy stood behind them and once again gave a nudge.

Instinctively moving forward after the second poke in her back, Jo looked up at the man beside her who was still calling after the TV guy. "Do you know what's going on?"

He bobbed his head. "I'm afraid so."

Odd response. "Is this for real?"

His steps slowed. "The show?"

"That and the money?"

Dylan blew out a long sigh and nodded again. "Again, I'm afraid so."

Having caught up to the man in charge, he grabbed each of their hands and slid hers into Dylan's. "Make nice for the camera. That's an order." He turned his back on them. "Okay, ready, set, and action."

This Dylan fellow was not only as irritated as she'd been, but she'd just noticed was also tall and rather good-looking, and had turned toward the man shouting orders. "This is ridi—"

"Wait a minute," she cut him off. "Would I have to sleep with you or something?"

The way his head snapped around and his eyes almost fell out of its sockets as he muttered, "What? No. I mean…"

He blew out a sigh and raised his gaze skyward, muttering, *"Serves me right. Of all the…"*

She suddenly didn't feel near as panicked as she had when she thought she was about to wind up on the human auction block. As a matter of fact, an odd sense of adrenaline shimmied up her spine at the thought of television, a good-looking guy, and a lot of money. What an adventure! "Let's do it."

"What?" The stunned solitary word wasn't quite the enthusiastic response she'd hoped for, but hey, even she knew the whole idea was a bit crazy.

"Let's win some money!"

Surely Dylan was having one of those ridiculous dreams a person had after eating bad leftover Chinese food. The whole idea of agreeing to do a reality dating TV show was insane enough, doing it with Colleen who had never been anything more than a best buddy only made the idea a little less absurd. Doing a romance show with a total stranger, even if she was rather pretty, had to be a bizarre dream.

"You guys are supposed to be in love, remember?" Carson shouted from across the narrow swath of deck.

From what Dylan could see, one couple, a cute short redhead and a tall skinny guy with glasses, were truly smitten. The sappy grin in their faces as they stared into each other's eyes was sort of sweet. The folks to his left looked as awkward as he felt. Apparently transferring online romance to in person love wasn't all that easy—real or not.

A lazy smile on her face, the blonde nestled at his side turned to face him. Staring into his eyes with an intensity the camera would probably love, her lips parted. "I suppose we should start with introductions. I'm Jo."

"Dylan." How crazy was this woman to agree on replacing Colleen with nothing more than prize money dangled in front of her? Granted, a lot of prize money, but no guarantees. "You don't have to do this." He wasn't even sure he had to do this.

"I was the lead in the high school play my junior and senior year. If you'll drop the frown and try to smile, we got this."

Not till that moment did he realize he'd been frowning at her. Forcing the corners of his mouth to tip upwards, he spoke through his teeth. "Better?"

An unexpected laugh erupted as she tipped her head back and laid her hand flat over his heart. "You may need a little more dress rehearsal."

Whether she was honestly amused or playing a part, he had no idea. What he did know is that this stranger had the deepest blue eyes he'd ever seen, and if his guess was right, the sun-kissed blonde hair was not out of a bottle.

"Start with your hands." Her gaze remained fixed on his.

"Hands?"

"Those are the two things at your side dangling on the ends of your arms."

He couldn't help it, the way she explained the obvious concept made him crack his first sincere smile of the day.

"There you go. Now, put them on my hips."

"Your hips?"

"Didn't you take biology in high school? Those are the things above my—"

"I know what hips are." Feeling like a pubescent boy at his first boy-girl party, he slowly settled one hand on her hip. Somehow placing both hands on a woman he'd known all of thirty minutes seemed all sorts of wrong.

"That's a start." The smile remained intact on her face.

A horn blew overhead and Carson's sidekick hollered, "Face the railing and wave."

Relieved to be out of the spotlight, Dylan shifted his feet and turned to face the railing, letting his arm fall to his side as he waved mindlessly with the other.

"People in love are always touching." She spoke while looking straight ahead.

He dared tear his gaze away from the port slipping

away. "Touching?"

Blowing out a heavy puff of air, she tipped her head sideways and stared up at him. "Am I only going to get one word commentaries out of you the whole trip?"

Afraid to give the monosyllabic answer of *no*, he shook his head.

"This may be harder than I thought." Without another word, the hand almost touching his, inched closer and threaded her fingers with his.

Oddly enough, out of all the insanity of the last few days, her delicate hand in his was the only thing that felt right. How crazy was that?

CHAPTER FOUR

"And, that's a wrap."

No longer in the camera's eye, Jo took a step back and studied the man in front of her. "So, let's see if I've got this right. You and your girlfriend are signed up for a reality show."

"Yes and no."

Just what she loved, a straight answer. "Feel free to expound on that."

"Yes, we're signed up for the TV show. No, she's not my girlfriend."

Jo let his words sink in. "I'm not following."

"Look." He glanced over his shoulder and back. "Let's find Colleen and your friends—"

"My sisters. Well, two are sisters."

"Fine. Let's find whoever and I'll explain it all more clearly."

Before she could answer either way, he'd turned on his heel and was working his way through the crowd like a native New Yorker on a subway platform.

"Where'd you go?" Mina stood with her hands on her hips, elbows out like chicken wings. "Poor Colleen is in her room refusing to go to the doctor."

"Who?" Jo asked at the same time Dylan muttered, "Blast. So she felt well enough to make it to the room?"

Mina stuck her hand out at Dylan. "I'm Mina, Jo's sister."

"Dylan Barnes. Nice to meet you. Where's Colleen?"

"My sister Ginnie and neighbor Angela took her down to her room. We," she wave her thumb over her shoulder, "my cousin Teresa and my maid of honor Brenda, waited here for you two to return. Where did you go?"

"Long story. I'll explain later." Jo didn't want to add, later after Dylan had fully explained to her what she'd gotten into.

"I need to check on her." Dylan was looking over Mina's shoulder toward the elevators before glancing back at Jo. "But we need to talk."

"Agreed." She took a step forward. "I'll come with you."

It took him a moment, but lips pressed tightly together, he gave a curt nod.

"Hold up." The man who'd been barking orders and introduced himself as Carter waved at them.

Dylan shook his head. "Not now. Colleen is really sick. I need to check on her."

Earlier the man's expression had been one of all business with a layer of stress, now all she could see was concern in his eyes. "Seasick or sick sick?"

"I don't know," Dylan sidestepped the crowd, "but I need to go now. If you want to talk you'll have to follow us."

The guy nodded and fell in step behind her, with her sister's entourage only a few feet behind him. Not quite the way she'd expected to start this cruise, but she had hoped for an adventure, and so far, this certainly fit the bill.

Once inside the ship, the halls had people going every which way and the elevator was packed. No one said a word. Even in the hall to Colleen's cabin, the single file line of people concerned about Colleen remained perfectly silent. At the door first, Dylan knocked.

One of the women from on deck opened the door and swung it wide open. "Oh, hello. I'm Ginnie."

"Thank you for helping Colleen."

"She's stubborn." The woman shook her head.

Only a moment later he realized where Colleen was.

The horrid sound of someone retching came through the bathroom door.

"Angela's in there with her. She began heaving the second the ship started moving. I say we call the doctor no matter how much she protests," Ginnie insisted.

It took a few seconds to realize everyone in the now crowded cabin was staring at him. Apparently, the final decision was his. Sucking in a deep breath, he nodded. "Let's call the doctor."

On the phone, as soon as he explained Colleen couldn't stop retching long enough to leave the bathroom, never mind make it below to the infirmary without soiling the shiny ship, the person on the other end agreed to send the doctor for a cabin-call.

"He should be here any minute," Dylan informed his audience as he hung up the desk phone.

"So," Ginnie, now sitting next to Jo on the twin bed, looked at him, "you and Colleen are on a TV show."

"Not anymore." Carson shook his head and pointed to Jo. "Now it's her and him."

Four heads whipped around to stare at Jo, but it was Mina who almost screeched, "What?"

Jo nodded and Dylan figured if they were all traveling together, then they all needed to know what was going on. He turned to Carson. "Maybe you should explain."

The man actually had the nerve to straighten his shoulders, puff out his chest, and smile at the women. "I'm the associate producer for a new reality game show, *Love on Deck*. The idea is that couples who meet and fall in love online, come together in person for the first time on this cruise ship. There will be several challenges they'll have to accomplish each day and the goal is whoever is still together and has the most audience votes by the end of the show will win a cash prize."

When he stopped talking, pretty much everyone in the room nodded.

"So you and Colleen met online?" Mina seemed to be the spokesperson for the group.

"No." Dylan shook his head. "We've been friends since

college. Just good friends."

Jo swung around and waved a finger at Carson. "But he said…"

"Yes. We had another contestant who pulled out at the last minute. Dylan and Colleen stepped in to save my hide. Besides," he shrugged, "they've been friends forever, maybe…"

"What?" Dylan spun around to face his friend. "Are you nuts?" He held up his hand. "Never mind, I already know the answer. You are nuts."

Carson held both his hands up, palms out. "Hey, it was just a thought."

A rap sounded on the door and Dylan pushed to his feet. "You and I will have a chat later."

A few minutes later, they managed to get Colleen out of the bathroom and onto the bed. While the doctor examined her, everyone else waited outside in the hall. No one said a word about the show. Without warning them, they all seemed to have understood the current situation shouldn't be overheard by passersby.

What seemed like forever but had actually only been several minutes, the doctor came out of the room and closed the door behind him. "I gave her something to help with the nausea. Hopefully she'll feel better in about twenty-four hours. If she doesn't, there might be something else at play besides the ship's movement."

Dylan nodded. "Thank you. Is there anything else we should do?"

"Just let her rest. Limit her meals for today to bananas, crackers, and a little broth. Sleep will be her friend."

"How do you sleep if you're throwing up?" Ginnie asked.

The doctor actually chuckled. "I gave her something to help her sleep too. Lying down will help. Trying to balance yourself when you're seasick makes the nausea worse."

"Thank you," Dylan repeated. Everyone stood still, watching the man walk down the hall and out of sight.

"Okay." Carson turned and looked to Dylan. "I suggest you two get a little better acquainted, there will be a champagne reception tonight—no cameras—and tomorrow we begin."

Before Dylan could respond, Carson turned and walked away.

"So you're going to go through with this?" Mina looked to her sister.

Jo shrugged. "The grand prize is two hundred and fifty thousand dollars."

Her eyes popped open wide, Ginnie nodded. "If I know my sister, and I do, dangle the promise of adventure in front of her and she's all in. Yep. She's doing it."

Once again all eyes were on him. With Colleen not well, not to mention she was the one who wanted the prize money, he just didn't know. Then again, he wasn't at all sure how big a mess his backing out would create for Carson. Blast, why couldn't life be simple?

CHAPTER FIVE

"**H**ave you lost your ever-loving mind?" Across the table from Jo, her sisters Mina and Ginnie looked like a matching set of bookends. Jo was blonde and blue-eyed and her sisters were dark-haired and dark-eyed. All three had similar features and mannerisms, but their difference in coloring always threw people off.

Mina and Ginnie had their father's coloring and Jo her mom's. On the other hand, Mina and Ginnie had their mother's temper and it was showing up now.

"I don't think so." At least not so far. She and Dylan were meeting after dinner. By dessert she'd have a better answer for her sisters, but for now, she'd gotten nothing but solid vibes from the guy. She also got the feeling he didn't really want to be doing this show, though there was always the chance she'd gotten that and everything else wrong.

"You don't think so?"

Two people walked by giggling. "Do you believe it? We're going to get to see a television show live. How cool is that?"

Everyone at the table watched the couple walk away.

"What's Mama going to say?" Ginnie plucked at the slice of pineapple on the rim of her glass.

"Oh dear." Jo shifted in her seat. "I hadn't thought of that." She really hadn't. It could go one of two ways, either her mother would be thrilled to death that another one of her daughters was actively seeking love—in which case she'd be horribly crushed to learn it was all pretend. Or, she'd go apoplectic that her youngest daughter would stoop so low, overlooking all the great Italian catches in their circle of friends. This time delighted it wasn't for real. "Still. I think if I win any part of that two hundred and fifty thousand dollars, Mama will forgive me anything. As long as I tell her before the show airs. I mean, some things simply needed to be explained face to face."

"Is this thing live?" Angie asked.

Jo had no idea. But she got where Angie was going with it. The more she thought about her mother's reaction, the more confused Jo became over what to do. If her mother saw the show not knowing it was all pretend, what kind of heart attack would she have believing Jo was in love for the whole world to see but hadn't told her mother? However she needed to handle it, she was sure of one thing, telling her mother over the phone would not go over well. "I'd better find out. If it is, we may have a problem."

"We?" Mina's brows shot up high on her forehead. "I won't be the one on a live television show."

"We don't know if it's live. Yet."

"Hmm," Ginnie huffed. "I don't know that the money is worth hiding something from Mama.

Jo simply rolled her eyes at her sister. Her mother's sixth, seventh, and eighth sense was part of the current dilemma.

"Hey." Brenda looked up. "What time were you supposed to meet with this guy?"

Jo looked down at her watch. "Oh, crud. In five minutes." She pushed to her feet. "Gotta run. See you guys later!"

The good thing about this ship was even though it was a little bigger than the previous one she and her sisters had sailed on, it had a very similar layout. Finding the piano bar would be easy, locating Dylan in the crowds of vacationing guests, partying their first night onboard, not so much.

Standing at the edge of the seating area, she scanned the tables and chairs, searching for the man who might be her fiancé for the next ten days and nights.

"Hello," the deep timbre of a man's voice against her back sent chills down her spine and her heart galloping. Whether he'd scared the heck out of her, or sparked something much deeper and a heck of a lot more frightening, she wasn't quite sure.

Quickly spinning around and taking a step back, she felt an upholstered seat press against her back, her feet stumble over themselves and strong hands gripping her arms to steady her.

"Sorry. Didn't mean to startle you."

Shaking her head, she gathered her wits, brushed the sides of her dress, and plastered on a smile. "No, no. The chair has a lot of nerve jumping up behind me."

The corners of his mouth lifted in a short chuckle. Going for levity had worked. "Shall we find a seat?"

Jo looked around. The place was packed. She hadn't checked the schedule to see why so many people were here. Not spotting a single empty chair, she turned, craning her neck to see the other side of the lounge, when one of the crew came onto the stage and announced the beginning of the Him and Her games. "Well, that explains a lot."

"It does?"

"It's a battle of the sexes type game and very popular."

"How much of a battle?" His gaze bounced over her shoulder to the man on stage.

"Fun stuff. Or at least it's supposed to be."

They stood in silence, watching a group of five men and five women shoving balloons under a large t-shirt. The objective was for the team with the most balloons under the shirt got the points.

"I wonder if this is the sort of thing Carson means when he says challenges?"

She shrugged. So far, she didn't know much of anything. "There!" Her finger stretched forward and pointed at two seats a few table away, where the couple had gathered their belongings and were walking away.

At the table they ordered a couple of drinks, watched the different teams go from running back and forth with an egg and passing it off, to running with a balloon between their knees and then having to sit on it till it popped.

"This had so better not be what Carson has in mind." Dylan shook his head.

For the majority of the game, they'd barely said a word, but she already knew they agreed on one thing. She didn't mind a little competition, but most of these bordered on sheer stupidity. In the end, the men's team won and within minutes, the crowds stood and moved on to another location and event.

"Now." She held her fruity drink between her hands and stared up at him. "Tell me what I'm in for?"

If only he knew. "I wonder if anyone knows. I've been friends with Carson all my life and he's being very tight-lipped."

"Wait. You and the TV guy are friends?"

He nodded.

"I thought that wasn't allowed?"

"That's what I had hoped." From the look in her eyes, he knew that last comment threw her. "I sort of got roped into this out of Carson's desperation and Colleen's enthusiasm. The idea of buying a house or paying off a mortgage holds a lot of appeal to people."

"It would to me."

"You own your own house? That's great."

"Not you?"

"Thought about it, but I don't want a condo in the city and commuting from the suburbs is a long haul in days that are already too long. Anyhow, I brought up the same question about friends of people involved in the show. Apparently, whatever attorney drew up the contracts was either asleep at the wheel or drunk on the job. There were plenty of provisions for family both by blood and marriage, but not a word about friends."

"So here you are?"

"Here I am." He nodded.

Jo stared down at her glass, swirling the pink contents, but not taking a sip. "How is Colleen doing?"

"Whatever the doctor gave her must be working. She woke up long enough to drink a little broth and went back to sleep."

"Does she know what's going on?"

"Yeah." He nodded. "I caught her up while she slurped the five spoonfuls of soup. She looked at me and very clearly suggested that throwing her overboard held more appeal than competing on a game show right about now."

Jo sputtered a suppressed laugh. "I think I like her. A sense of humor is important in life."

"And she certainly has one."

"So are we doing this?"

"I don't know. I told her I'd split my share with her if we win, but—"

"No. I wouldn't have this opportunity if she hadn't been involved in the first place. *We'll* split the prize three ways."

"That's if we win."

A sly smile teased at one side of her mouth. "When we win."

"You seem awfully confident."

She shrugged. "Like I said, I'm a pretty good actress. As for the rest of the challenges, I'm surmising if they haven't made anyone sign releases for injuries or given us pysch evals, then whatever they come up with won't require boot camp first."

"I'm not sure which would be worse, swimming through a snake-infested river carrying a bag of rocks or a pie-eating contest with my hands behind my back."

"If it's coconut cream it would be a no brainer."

That made him laugh. Maybe she really was a nut; at least she was an amusing nut, and he suspected, more likely, a good sport.

For what he thought was the next half hour or so, they'd exchanged as much basic information as they considered likely to have been shared online while courting. That, of course, included his first day of school when he told the teacher he wasn't motivated to learn, and Jo's story about painting her cousin Giovanni, better known to all as Joe's, toenails in bubblegum-pink nail polish while he was sleeping. Something he didn't discover until he took his socks off at the lake in front of his friends.

The real surprise was discovering their half hour or so

conversation had extended into well over two hours. Maybe, if they were both lucky, this entire cruise show thing would fly by just as fast. He looked up and spotted his friend and other members of the crew at a larger table across the lounge. The way they all had their heads together and suddenly burst out in choral laughter, his stomach took a nose dive and he knew as sure as his name was Dylan Allen Barnes, this was going to be one very long cruise.

CHAPTER SIX

"**H**ave they lost their minds?" Ginnie flung her arm over her eyes and mumbled at Jo.

"Trust me." She tripped over one sandal in search of the other. "Had I been told that the show started with breakfast at seven in the morning, I wouldn't have signed up."

"You can still back out. Everyone would understand." The arm hadn't moved.

Not everyone. She'd be letting Colleen down, Carson down—not that she knew him well enough to care, but she did—and maybe even Dylan. Even though she barely knew any of them, she couldn't bring herself to give up without even trying. "I'll be gone in a minute."

A sound somewhere between a huff and a grunt filled the small cabin as her sister rolled over and pulled the covers over her head. Ginnie muttered something else that may have been *enjoy breakfast* or *don't fall off the boat*—who knew which.

Stepping into one shoe, she danced out the front door, trying to slip on the other sandal and pull the door closed at the same time. She'd intended to get out the door early, have some time to get to know the ship, maybe meet the other contestants before the official gathering, but that idea flew out the window when she hit the snooze button. Stabbing at the elevator button, she hurried down to the private conference room the show had requested for their first breakfast.

"Morning." The couple who had looked like ready to devour each other with their eyes on deck the afternoon before smiled at her. To Jo's chagrin, they looked just as hungry for each other this morning. She was torn between the thought of how sweet and the reality that this was their competition for a quarter of a million dollars. Her cute meter crumbled.

The other couple had yet to arrive, but Dylan stood stiffly just inside the doorway to the conference hall. "Good morning." He waved toward one of three sweetheart tables. At least she assumed that was the intent. Like the bride and groom table at a wedding reception rather than a dais for the entire bridal party. Clearly, the folks in charge of the show didn't want the couples too close—yet.

"Good morning." Carson turned away from a huddle with this staff in the corner and smiling at the two couples, moved to the front of the room. "As soon as Sandy and Jay … ah, here they are. Take your seats. While breakfast is served, I shall explain the plan for the day."

The third couple didn't crack even a hint of a smile. They quietly moved to the empty table, the man's hand barely guiding her from the small of her back. They didn't look very happy to be in this situation. The image made Jo very aware of how appearances might affect the viewing public and judges on the ship. If there were judges on the ship.

"I'm sure by now you've all had time to read over the game rules that have been sent to you."

Jo's gaze bounced over to Dylan. She hadn't been given anything. Of course she was a very last-minute addition. Still, from the narrowing of Dylan's eyes, she would guess he hadn't read anything either.

"You'll notice you've been given a call sheet. You will only be mic'd and on camera for those scheduled scenes."

That gave her a moment of relief. She'd feared the filming would be 24/7 and she would have to sneak away somehow to spend any time with her sisters and friends. After all, the real reason for her trip was her sister, and no amount of money would be enough for her to disappoint Mina on the verge of the most important day of her life.

"There will be a cameraman following you at a discreet distance at all times, but you will only be mic'd according to the call sheet schedule. Expect it to take half an hour or so to mic you at the start and then again to remove the mics when we're done. Please note the cameraman will not be filming you every hour of the day, but if I or one of the other production crew notices something that will be of value to the show, the camera might start rolling. In other words, your only true private sanctuary for the next nine days will be in your cabins." Carson chuckled. "And, of course, the restrooms."

A few heads turned to eye their significant other, but mostly everyone nodded. The reality of what they were getting into had probably just smacked most people in the face.

"Now." Grinning, Carson slapped his hands together enthusiastically. "You will see on the tables your first challenge of the show."

There were two of them at the table, but only one packet of information. Leaning back to allow the waiter to slip a dish of eggs, bacon, and toast in front of her, she then leaned forward to go over the sheets Dylan already held in his hand.

"As you know, most reality shows have official judges ruling on the daily events. We're a little different. The passengers on the ship will be the official judges. All of them." He waited for that information to settle in before continuing. "We will, of course, have television viewer participation, and one or two, or more," his eyes sparkled with knowing something no one else knew, "events will require professional judges."

Jo really wanted to raise her hand and insist on being told what kind of professional judges. If it meant getting on ice, or making sushi, she was in trouble. Now if there was a fresh pasta making competition, she was a shoe-in.

"You will see the first challenge of this competition will begin one hour after breakfast today. The theme, your new home."

"We have a new home?" she whispered to Dylan.

Glancing at her quickly, his brows rose high and his lips tipped down in what she could only describe as a facial shrug.

"You will be working from stations in the Captain's lounge. It does not officially open until five pm, so you'll have pretty much all day to assemble your furniture."

That sounded easy enough. Maybe.

"Each station will have one dresser," Carson continued, "one recliner, and one swing."

Three pieces. She already knew she hated directions, preferred just using common sense, but this was no time to jettison the data from those who knew more than she did. Hopefully, Dylan was better at following instructions than she was.

Carson took a step forward. "You may wander upstairs if you like. Look at the boxes. But no peeking at instructions until the official race time."

"Race?" one of the contests muttered to themselves, but the group heard it nonetheless.

"Didn't I mention that?" Carson smiled. "Points will be awarded for the best-looking finished project, the best display of cooperation, and of course, the fastest completion time. So, enjoy your breakfast, when you're done, the fun will begin."

Carson bobbed his head at everyone as if he had just made a royal proclamation and rejoined his crew at the large table nearby. Jo turned to Dylan and through a forced smile, softly uttered, "Please tell me you know what to do with a screwdriver that doesn't have vodka or orange juice."

Dylan would have preferred to be given piles of lumber and told to create something beautiful than to have to assemble do-it-yourself furniture, but even though he was a lawyer, he did indeed know the difference between a flathead and a Phillips head screwdriver. "I do."

"I don't like reading instructions written by foreign engineers who don't know their left from their right, but if I can decipher a technical manual, I can decipher furniture hieroglyphics. I hope." All he did was dip his chin once in agreement and her eyes took on an unexpected sparkle. "We're going to nail this, aren't we?"

He gave her a casual shrug, but couldn't help the grin that tugged at his lips. "We'll have to see, but I'm optimistic."

Shaking her head, she chuckled softly. "Sure you're a lawyer and not a doctor?"

"Positive." So far, this morning was starting out better than he'd feared. Before arriving at breakfast, he'd taken a moment for one last check on Colleen. Leaving the adjoining door unlocked had made it easier for him to sleep, knowing he would hear if she needed anything. At least once in the middle of the night he'd heard the toilet flush and felt relief that she was not heaving up her lunch anymore, nor falling down in a weakened state. This morning, she'd reassured him all was well and room service was a breeze. Then she told him to break a leg, rolled over, and was snoring before he'd latched the cabin door closed behind him.

Considering the three participating couples were supposed to be lovebirds, except for the chatter from the crew table, the room was mostly silent. Occasionally a knife or fork would clank against a plate, but few words were spoken between the six contestants. Even he and Jo had simply eaten their food and then excused themselves.

Outside, crossing the ship on deck instead of via an interior corridor, she slowed her steps. "It occurs to me that we're going to have to think a few things through here." Glancing at his hands, she reached for one.

The unexpected touch almost had him jumping out of his skin.

"Did you notice that one couple look ready to pounce on each other and the other couple looks to be afraid of their own shadow?"

He had. "I almost think they regret getting into this mess."

"Exactly. Which means, if the entire ship will be our official judges, then we have to look, at the very least, like we like each other pretty much all the time."

Understanding where her point was leading, he held up their now clasped hands. "Little things like holding hands."

She tapped her nose with her free hand. "Give the man a prize."

What he really needed was a stronger cup of coffee. Maybe, even if it was only nine in the morning, an Irish coffee—or two. He'd never had to play the part of a man in love, and heaven help him, he didn't know if he had it in him. He bobbed his head at her. "You're right. Holding hands from time to time is a good idea."

A smile took over her face, and once again he spotted a twinkle in her eye. "We can do this."

They walked the remaining distance to the area the show had roped off for them, hand in hand. The feeling wasn't quite natural, but at least she no longer felt like a perfect stranger. Spotting the sections with the unpacked boxes, he looked for any assignment of areas. "Do you think we get to choose our spot?"

She shrugged. "No clue."

A few moments later, the couple who already looked like newlyweds walked up beside them. The guy turned and stuck out his hand at Dylan. "I'm Colin, this is Debbie."

The redhead turned slowly, obviously more hesitant than her counterpart. If Dylan were a betting man, he'd say Colin was the extravert of the pair. "Nice to meet you. I'm Dylan and this is Jo."

Small talk was made until the third couple, Jay and Sandy, joined them. From what he could see, neither would be considered an extravert, and he had his doubts if these two even liked each other. Almost made Dylan wonder if they were another pair of ringers like him and Jo.

"I see you're all here." Carson came walking up behind them. "There are no assigned spaces. You can pick whichever spot you want."

Dylan scanned the area. From what he could see, the three sections were side by side in a single row and there did not appear to be one advantage over the other. He turned to Jo. "Have a preference?"

She shrugged. "Not really. Might as well take the one

on the left. More people will see us. Maybe we can develop a fan base."

Fan base? Jo clearly had a better grasp of the politics of reality television than he did. Taking a second glance, Jay and Sandy weren't making a move but Colin and Debbie were deep in conversation as if positioning was key to winning or losing. Unless they wanted to spend the next ten days debating what the six of them were doing next, Dylan took a step in the direction Jo had suggested, and gently tugging her to his side, claimed the section. Now all they had to do was build some pretty furniture, look like an enamored couple, and do it all faster than the next guy. Piece of cake. He considered if his playing the lottery like Colleen didn't have better odds.

CHAPTER SEVEN

How hard could any of this be? So far, all was going well. If Jay and Sandy kept their frosty distance, they were as good as at the bottom of the scoreboard. Assuming the show actually used a scoreboard. They had to have scoreboard, how else would they keep track?

"Something wrong?" Dylan asked softly, his gaze bouncing between Jo and the boxes.

"No. Just thinking." She hadn't meant to stand there frowning. Her mother had always told her she had too expressive a face and would make a lousy poker player. Once, she had a teacher who confessed that she always dummied down the class to the level of the most confused student. The choices she made were based on the student's facial expressions. Jo was so expressive that the teacher would watch Jo and when she made funny faces, the teacher would repeat herself or switch up how she said something. It had taken the woman almost an entire semester to realize that Jo's expressions rarely had anything to do with what the teacher had been explaining. Now especially, she would have to try and figure out how to hide her own thoughts.

Together, they opened the first box. The dresser.

Dylan pulled out the bag of parts. "We'll start with the largest project. Then we can better judge how we're doing for time."

Made sense to Jo. She helped pull the pieces out of the box, carefully sorting by size and making sure not to lose the small pieces, then glanced over at Dylan. "What are you doing?"

"Reading the instructions." His eyes didn't lift from the page.

"Be still my heart. A man reading instructions?"

This time his gaze lifted from the papers in his hand and met hers. "It happens." He folded the pages and set them to one side.

"Want me to read them to you as we go?" She started to reach over to grab the instructions.

"No need."

"So you are a man?"

"Excuse me?" For the second time in as many moments, he stopped what he was doing and looked up at her.

"You have very nice eyes." She hadn't meant to say that out loud and instinctively her hands flew to her mouth. Apparently, she was going to have to add her mouth to the list of things she needed to be careful with. "Sorry. Didn't mean to say that."

"So I don't have nice eyes?" Now those chocolate-brown eyes with a hint of caramel flecks were smiling at her.

She sat back on her heels and returned the smile. "You do."

"Thank you." He paused another moment. Opened his mouth, then closed it, then opened it again.

"What?"

He shook his head and pointed to the long piece of wood beside her. "Hand me that, please."

Nodding, she did as she was told, and for the next short while, they worked in near silence, only exchanging a few words like *that one*, *the long one*, *over there, hold this please,* and a few times, one or both of them mumbled a simple *hmm.*

He reached for a long board and Jo glanced at the instructions on the ground beside her. "I don't think that goes there."

"I know, but this will reinforce the back better if we put it lower than the diagram."

Engineering and mechanics weren't part of her skill sets, but even she could see the logic in his choice. "Not bad for a lawyer."

His smile slipped and a light crease formed between his brows. She had no idea if that was because of the project or what she'd just said. Maybe time would tell. Or maybe she was over thinking the whole thing. While Dylan placed the last pieces of bracing onto the dresser frame, she screwed the drawer glides in place. A few more minutes and the dresser was complete, looked good, and … darn. Colin and Debbie were gleefully opening another box, their completed porch swing and cover looking pretty beside them. She should have known a man with glasses would be able to translate instructions easily. Though construction skills surprised her. And yet, how many times had her mother told her not to judge a book by its cover.

"You're frowning again."

It took all of her self-control not to roll her eyes. Not at him, at herself. Apparently controlling her facial expressions was even harder for her Italian genetics than not talking with her hands. She was definitely going to have to concentrate more. "They finished the first piece before us."

Dylan glanced over at the other couple. Slowly, as his gaze examined their opponent's project, that lazy smile reappeared. "Let's get back to work. We have two more pieces to build."

Of course, he was right. They hadn't lost the round to speed yet. She grabbed the scissors to open a new box and noticed that Jay and Sandy were still working on the desk. Funny how each couple had started with a different piece, but what caught her eye was how the two appeared to be falling way behind. Rather than feeling relief at being ahead of at least one of the couples, all she felt was awful that they were struggling. She wanted to win, but not till this second did she realize that meant someone else would have to lose. And why did that have to bother her so much?

Dylan still would have preferred to make his own furniture, but putting the do-it-yourself project together had been way more fun than he would have thought. Though he wasn't ready to accept the probability, yet, that the fun was not in the project but the company.

Opening the desk box next, they made quick work of the assembly. As he'd done with the previous box, he quickly perused the instructions, looking for any red flags and getting a general idea of how the manufacturer intended for it to be put together.

Moments before they attached the covering on the patio swing they'd successfully assembled, Colin and Debbie bounced with delight.

Meanwhile, a dresser drawer in her lap, Sandy's expression reminded him of his sister when she was ten years old and ready to cry after he'd taken away her favorite doll.

"Darn," Jo muttered.

His gaze darted back to the happy couple bouncing in place. And the patio swing behind them. Squinting, he looked more closely at the finished product and had to bite back a chuckle. "Not yet."

Jo's gaze followed the direction he was staring in. Leaning in so close that her breath nearly tickled his ears, she asked, "What are you talking about?"

The words were barely out of her mouth when the happy couple sank onto their swing set and crashed onto the carpeted floor.

"Oh, my." Jo's hand flew to her mouth.

Dylan leaned against her. "They didn't screw the cover through the whole thing, only across the top. I guess they didn't realize that without the larger knob and screw, the seat wouldn't hold their weight."

Just to show what he meant, he discreetly pointed to the knob in the main hole instead of the top hole for height adjustment, then, taking her hand, sat her down beside him.

"Well, well, folks." A man Dylan had yet to meet and who he assumed was the show's host, stood shaking his head. "Looks like finishing before the others isn't going to get you enough points for first place."

Now, the guests who had been standing around the

contestants for pretty much the whole morning it had taken to put all the pieces together, were allowed to cross the velvet rope and examine the work, and handed a paper and pen to rank the best finished product, and who they thought had worked best together.

By now, Jay and Sandy had finished placing the drawers in the dresser and had taken a seat on the outdoor swing. The two were still not touching, or sitting close, which reminded Dylan of what Jo had said before. Without saying a word, he reached over and took her hand in his, and pushing off with his foot, set the patio seat to swinging. Of course there was no view of the ocean where he lived, but overall, he liked the idea of rocking on the back porch with a partner beside him. Really liked it.

"All right, ladies and gentlemen," the host announced into the lounge PA system. "For the fastest time segment, we have couple number one, Dylan and Jo, in first place with three points, Jay and Sandy in second with two points, and disqualified for incomplete work, Colin and Debbie have zero points. Of course, this is still the first day and the first challenge, there will be plenty of opportunity for the numbers to shift."

"Uh, oh." Jo elbowed him.

"What?"

With her chin, she pointed in the direction of Colin and Debbie. Having gotten up from the floor, Debbie seemed to be clenching her teeth and holding back a few choice words. Another second and Colin stepped in close, smiled at his newfound love, brushed a lock of hair behind her ear, and just like that, the two were once again fluttering around each other like a pair of smitten butterflies. "Never mind. Just wishful thinking."

"And we now have the tally of votes for best finished product and best-working team." The guy counted off, and in the end, as with the first announcement, the placement was he and Jo in first, Jay and Sandy second and Colin and Debbie last, though they had beat out Jay and Sandy in the best teamwork points. "Join us this afternoon as the contestants gather once again for a little game of music relay."

"What the heck is that?" Jo asked.

Dylan shrugged. Music wasn't a scary subject for him. He was actually pretty diverse in his tastes. Studying for college exams and later law school, there was always music in the background with variety dating back to his grandfather's generation. "No clue. But so far, none of this is making me nervous."

"You were nervous?" She hadn't let go of his hand or stopped the seat from swinging.

He hid a smile. "Maybe. A little."

"Good. I thought I was the only one."

"Looking good." Carson came up behind them and slapped Dylan on the back. Quickly he glanced over his shoulder before leaning in. "You guys look like a real couple. Well done."

Before either of them could say a word, Carson had moved on to offer what Dylan assumed were words of encouragement to the other contestants.

"Do you think the whole thing is going to be this easy?" Jo kept her gaze on Carson's back and the other couples.

He hefted one shoulder in a half-hearted shrug. "No, idea." He certainly hoped so, but something inside told him fat chance.

CHAPTER EIGHT

"Would you chew before swallowing, please." Jo's sister Mina shook her head at the youngest of the Ummarino girls.

"I can't help it." Jo held the sandwich mid-air before setting it down to wipe her mouth. "I'm starving. Who knew competition could make you so hungry?"

Ginnie waved her thumb at Dylan. "He's in the competition too, and you don't see him shoveling food down his throat like a gorilla in a banana field."

Every single person at the large family table turned to look at Ginnie. Utter confusion and jaw-dropping surprise painted their faces.

"Where do you come up with these things." Jo picked a slice of salami out of her sandwich. "There isn't even such a thing as a banana field."

"You get my point." Ginnie waved a fork at her youngest sister before stabbing at her salad.

"So now what?" Angela reached for her fruit punch.

"Music challenge," Jo muttered around the sandwich against her lips.

"Oh." Their cousin Teresa sat up straighter. "I love music trivia shows."

Dylan leaned back in his seat. "I'm not sure it's trivia exactly. The host called it a music relay."

Her sister Mina frowned. "What the heck does that mean?"

"That," Jo set her half-eaten sandwich down, "is what we wondered."

At first, she and Dylan had thought to separate for lunch, but since the only other person he knew onboard was his friend Carson, and they were supposed to be in the blooms of new love for all passengers onboard to see, they decided it might be in their best interest to lunch together. Before meeting her sisters and friends, they'd stopped downstairs to check on Colleen.

She was feeling so much better that she'd decided to disregard the doctor's instructions to rest and got dressed, determined to find her old and new friends. By the time she'd showered and gotten her underwear on, it struck her, literally, that leaving the cabin was not a good idea at all. They'd found her drinking soup in bed, only a little green, and perfectly content to stay put while they battled on for the prize money.

"Since it's clear the production company intends to keep you too busy to hang out with us," Brenda dipped her fry in some ketchup, "we might as well check out what you're up to."

"Could be fun," Teresa shrugged.

Ginnie waved her hands in the air, palms up. "I really do like music trivia."

Shoveling the last bite of sandwich in her mouth, Jo shrugged and chewing quickly, swallowed. "Up to you guys."

Her friends and family looked from one to the other, nodded, and Mina turned back to her and Dylan. "I guess our first afternoon at sea will be listening to you guys do karaoke or trivia or whatever it turns out to be."

"As long as I don't have to play a trumpet, we're fine." Outnumbered by all the estrogen, Dylan simply smiled at his own bad joke.

They'd only spent an hour with the bachelorette entourage, but he seemed to be taking this being outnumbered thing really well. Considering the men in her own family were often overwhelmed when outnumbered by Ummarino women, she was truly impressed by his easygoing nature. The whole thing made her think maybe she should find a nice lawyer to date.

"Where is the next event?" Angela pushed away from the table. "I need to run to my room a minute."

"Same place. In the piano lounge." Jo took a long sip of iced tea. "What do you need to go all the way to your room for?"

"My phone, of course. Someone has to take pictures."

Brenda shook her head. "Video is better blackmail material."

The two women laughed and Jo nearly choked on her own spit. "You can't do that. What if Mom sees it?"

"I'm sorry," Mina stared at her sister as if she'd grown a third eye, "you do realize there's a real live film crew taking video of you, don't you?"

"Yes, but Carson confirmed it won't air until I'm home and can break Mom's television."

"Ha," Ginnie huffed. "Fat chance of that."

Her sisters were right. She'd have to figure this all out later. When she wasn't in the thick of things. But still. "No phones."

"Party pooper." Angela stuck her tongue out at Jo.

It didn't take long for everyone to gather what little belongings they'd carried with them and settle down with a front-row view of the anticipated events.

"Oh, good heavens." Teresa held her hand to her throat.

"What's wrong?" Jo looked at the table, but Teresa hadn't brought her drink or food, so she wasn't choking.

Her mouth was moving but no sound was coming out. Teresa's arm lifted and her finger pointed ahead to the host for the next challenge. "That's, that's … he's…"

"For the love of Henry," Mina rolled her eyes, "spit it out."

"Dirk Simpson."

"Who?" Jo asked.

"The host of that reality show about giving sick kids their wishes."

Jo spun around in her seat to pay closer attention to the guy. He was a little older and his hair a little shorter, but her cousin was right. The emcee for the challenges was the host for the new show. Leaning back in her seat, she blew out a long breath.

"Something wrong?" Dylan spoke softly, his hand

settling gently on her shoulder.

"No." She shook her head. "Just my mom's favorite host of her favorite show. No matter how you slice it, there will be no stopping her from watching our show. I am so screwed."

The way Jo had gone suddenly pale he wasn't sure if she'd caught Colleen's seasickness or was about to regurgitate her entire lunch and breakfast. From the look on her face, either of those options may have been better than having to deal with her mother. He didn't know the woman, but he had similar concerns about his colleagues. And clients. But he wasn't going to go there now.

"Welcome, welcome, ladies and gentlemen." Dirk stood at the front of a small stage. With every word he spoke, more passersby stopped to see what was going on.

"We have one part of a surprise for our contests this afternoon." He waved his arm at three couples strolling hand in hand onto the stage.

If not for their almost elegant appearance, formal attire, updo hairstyles, and enough makeup to hide anything and everything, Dylan might have thought they were additional contestants.

The man proceeded to introduce each couple by name as they stepped forward and did an appropriate curtsey or bow. "These are some of our top dancers from our ship's Broadway production. They are about to entertain you with a demonstration of the beloved," he lowered his voice, leaning into the mic, "and romantic," standing upright again, his voice rose, "Tango! Give them a hand."

For the next several minutes, Dylan watched the three couples sweep across the floor in various stages of the famed Argentine dance. When one of the men almost threw his partner across the floor, the entire audience gasped. Not until she spun about, legs turned on the wooden floor and sprang up again, did the room burst out in thunderous applause. Minute by minute each couple performed breathtaking moves. He couldn't imagine ever having the skillset to master such a sleek, sensual, and famous dance. When all three men lowered their dance partners into a final dip, most of the room was on their feet. Him included.

"Wow," Jo whispered to no one in particular. "Just wow."

"You took the words right out of my mouth." Ginnie clapped so hard and fast, Jo wouldn't have been surprised if her hands snapped off her arms.

"And now," Dirk continued, "if we could have our contestants on stage."

Dylan pushed to his feet and stretched out his arm to Jo before proceeding. The gesture seemed so natural. Like something they'd been doing for years. For her and Colleen's sake, he hoped the rest of the viewing audiences, both here and in TV land, agreed with him.

"For your dance relay." He paused and smiled at the growing audience. "Did I say music earlier?"

Several heads bobbed, and he repeated the question, this time getting the thunderous applause he was after.

"That's right," he boomed. "This is a dance relay. I have several traditional dances in this hat here." He held up a very large-brimmed cowboy hat. "The objective is that one partner will pull a paper out of the hat, and then, with no music accompaniment, the partner has three chances to guess the dance. If the couple doesn't guess it, then the next two couples can guess and win extra points."

That was not what Dylan had been expecting, and worse, as good as he was at music, he was equally abysmal at dance. Heaven help them. They all proceeded onto the stage at Dirk's prompting and were given the option of deciding who was the dancer and who was the guesser. Neither of them seemed particularly enthused about either role. As far as he could tell, with this one, they were both in deep trouble.

Besides drawing dances from the hat, there was an additional glass bowl that determined who went first. He was unsure if he wanted to go first and get it over with, or let someone else set the bar for the challenge. Though traditionally it might beg the question, how high? He was hoping for seriously low.

The first up was Colin and Debbie. He drew the paper, nodded, smiled, gave it to the host and proceeded to sway his hips, slap his hands across his chest, move them behind his head, make a funny squished expression with his face, which told Dylan he had no idea what to do next, and proving Dylan wasn't the only one thinking that, Dirk quickly added, "And no singing allowed. Not even a single line. If your partners know it, then they know it, otherwise, we'll work it all out. Soon." The contestant continued for a few minutes while Debbie shouted anything that came to mind including the well-known Twist and the Monster Mash. It was clear from the way she nibbled on her lower lip that she was not happy, nor did she have a clue what to guess.

As promised, as soon as the contestant's third guess had come on gone, the others were allowed to vote. Having been given an electronic clicker, Dylan quickly pressed the small fob, and waited for his name to be called. Since the other couple had made no effort to communicate, he called out 'Macarena' and had won a point for himself and Jo. With Colin seated beside her, Debbie had frowned and huffed, and let her frustration be known. In the end, as he had the challenge before, he'd made a sweet gesture and put the smile back on her face. The TV audience would probably eat that up.

Even with three dances per team member, time was passing much too quickly before it would be his and Jo's turn. What he had learned was that the Chicken Dance was way before anyone's time, and Debbie did a terrible Moonwalk. Perhaps had they given her a dark suit and white glove, someone might have guessed it, but the only thing that had made sense was when Jay shouted out the Stroll. Dylan didn't even know if that was a real dance or not.

No surprise, Jay had been the one to go first for their team. What had surprised him was how by the third dance,

Sandy had begun to shout out her guesses more quickly and even smiled when she'd correctly guessed the Electric Slide.

When Dylan and Jo's turn came along, he prayed for something simple and easily recognizable for any fool, like the Twist or the Charleston. No such luck. Who knew the Floss or Dougie were the names of dances? Certainly not Jo or him. In the end, they came in third. Hopefully, there would be no more dancing in their cruising future.

Dylan had never been so happy for anything to come to an end. He'd rather take the bar exam again than go through the humiliation of waving his arms around his head for the longest sixty seconds of his life. Though on second thought, flapping his arms like a fledgling bird debating flight might have been worse.

"And now," Dirk the host spoke into the mic, "we have something special for our contestants and guests."

Somehow, the word special lost all value when coming from the mouth of a reality game show host on a floating hotel.

"You remember the dancers from our entertainment crew?"

The thunderous applause that erupted told Dylan and Dirk that no one had forgotten the amazing dance presentation.

"Wonderful." The man in a snug fitting white suit grinned. "Starting tomorrow morning…"

Dylan closed his eyes and felt the fingers on Jo's hand that he'd been holding go cold.

"Each one of you will begin a week's dance lessons."

Okay, he breathed a sigh of relief. He'd survived cotillion at his mother's insistence. He could do this. Except Jo's hand had gone from chilled to ice cold.

"You'll learn to do this stunning tango and show off your talents on the last night of the cruise. And of course, there will be judges, but that's a surprise for another day. Isn't that wonderful, folks?"

Suddenly it dawned on Dylan that maybe his lifelong friendship with Carson wasn't such a big deal. So what if he ruined the man's life and career? His mother would forgive him for letting his best friend down. After all, she loved Dylan more. Maybe. From behind his shoulder, he could hear Jo's family's soft words of encouragement that ranged from a forced *could be worse* to an enthusiastic *how exciting*.

Daring to face his soon-to-be dance partner, Dylan could see the same doubts in her eyes that were churning in his gut and settling in his two left feet. This was most definitely not what he had in mind when the word *challenges* had been tossed around.

Learning to tango. Like the dancers in front of them dressed in bright red dresses and buttoned-up suits. What in the name of Frank Capra had they gotten themselves into?

CHAPTER NINE

"**W**ord is starting to get around." Jo looked out over the rail into the almost black sea under a star-filled night.

"I'm almost afraid to ask what word is that." Dylan stood at her side. Close enough for passersby to know they were together, far enough apart to respect each other's personal space.

"That we're part of the game show."

"Sort of hard to miss!" From the poolside lounge chair, Brenda shouted over her shoulder between sips of the ship's drink of the day. "Especially when that guy with the camera follows you everywhere."

Dylan chuckled. "She has a point."

"At least we get a little time to ourselves." Jo turned her eyes away from the ocean in time to catch Dylan staring at her with one brow cocked high on his forehead.

"You mean ourselves and a few hundred passengers." He took a second to look over his shoulder, past her family enjoying the late night movie outdoors, and scanned the hundreds of passengers spanning the lounge chairs, swimming pool, and deck walkers.

She shrugged. "Okay, maybe not totally to ourselves."

As if on cue, they both chuckled and rested their arms on the railing again.

"I think I'll have another." Brenda glanced around her and pushed to her feet.

Mina sucked up the last of her drink. "Me too."

"Shouldn't you two take it easy on those? They pack quite a punch." Ginnie was still only partway finished with hers.

"Why?" the two friends echoed, then burst into a fit of giggles like a couple of school girls.

"It's not like we have to drive," Brenda added.

"True," Ginnie shrugged, "but still."

"Wait. I'll go with them." Angela hopped up and patted Ginnie on the shoulder. "Just to make sure they find their way back," she teased.

That only made Jo and Dylan laugh a little harder.

After a few moments of heavy silence, still smiling, Dylan tipped his head in Jo's direction. "It's nice to laugh."

Also smiling, and feeling content with the evening moment, she nodded. "Yes, it is." Turning to face him, she leaned one elbow on the rail. "I gather you don't laugh often?"

"I'm a lawyer. I'm lucky I laugh ever."

"What does being a lawyer have to do with laughing?"

"We tend to see the ugly side of life. Doesn't matter what kind of lawyer you are. In corporate law there's always a cut-throat causing trouble for the little guy. In divorce, well, there's always infighting over money and kids, though from what I've heard folks fight more over the dog than the kids. The seedy side of life is obvious in criminal law. Then you have—"

Still smiling somehow, she cut him off, holding out her hand. "I get the picture. Sorry I asked."

"No. I'm sorry. The law has been a bit of a thorn in my side lately."

"Tell me about it."

The way he looked at her, almost as if seeing through her, made her wonder what was really behind this man who was playing a part for a prize he didn't seem that keen on wanting.

"It's presumed that law is part of the Barnes family DNA."

"Presumed?"

"All the first-born sons are expected to, and have, become lawyers."

"And you're the first-born son." It wasn't a question.

"I'm the only son." He paused a long moment before

continuing. "I have a younger sister."

"Oh, how much younger?"

"Only three years."

"Are you close?"

One side of his mouth twisted up in a gesture that did imply a resounding yes. "Sometimes it feels like we are, but I think that's just wishful thinking." He seemed to be considering something, or maybe considering how much to share. "I envy the way you and your sisters interact."

That gave her pause. They behaved like sisters. Nothing special. "How is that?"

"You tease each, joke around, and even pick on each other a little. Like Ginnie and Mina now over those fruity drinks. But, on the flip side, you take care of each other, protect each other, and have each other's backs."

"You concluded all that from five minutes of banter over an adult fruit punch?" Yes, everything he said was correct, but how he'd drawn that conclusion so quickly, with so little evidence, surprised her.

"Actually, it's a compilation of interactions since yesterday afternoon. For instance, both your sisters thought you were insane for agreeing to play the part of a newly in love couple with a man you'd just met, even for money, and yet, less than twenty-four hours later, there they were cheering you on."

Somewhere deep down, she'd just assumed they would support her no matter how crazy her idea might be. "I guess this would be where that thing about people in glass houses would come into play."

Dylan chuckled. "Don't throw stones?"

"Well, yes, but I was thinking more that the view for those looking in is different than for those looking out." She took in a long slow breath, considered her own thoughts, and slowly exhaled. "I guess I hadn't really thought about it that way. Being the youngest of the three, I'd spent most of my life feeling the need to catch up to my sisters. If I heard *wait till you're older* once, I heard it a thousand times. Even now, we're all working adults, and yet, it feels like mine is usually the last opinion to be taken seriously."

"I hadn't noticed."

She felt her brows crumple. "Why would you?"

"Everyone, including your neighbor and sister's friend, seemed to have an opinion on our situation, and yet," he shrugged, "your opinion won."

"I don't know that there was a choice in the matter. It's my life." A hint of a smile teased at the corners of her mouth. "And prize money."

"I rest my case."

"Sorry. What?"

"Your life, your choice, and maybe your money, but agree with you or not, here they are drinking, laughing, and tomorrow they'll be at the next challenge, cheering you on. They've happily given up most of their plans to share your new ones. And so far, they seem to be having fun."

"Yes. I think they are." She had to admit, he did have a point. Her sisters' support, no matter how crazy her idea, was something she'd always taken for granted. She couldn't imagine her life without them, even if half the time they thought she was just a little bit crazy.

"Besides," his mind quickly ran images of the three sisters laughing over the last day, "my money's on you have every intention of sharing your winnings with your family."

The way her eyes rounded and brows shot up on her forehead, he couldn't determine if he was spot on or dead wrong.

"Are you this good in a court of law?"

He shook his head. "I don't do litigation. But, yes, reading people and their intentions is key to successful negotiations. A good lawyer needs to know when they can push and when it's time to pick up their marbles and go home."

"And you're good?"

"Good enough."

"I feel like there's a but in there somewhere."

"My sister's better."

"She's a lawyer too?"

He nodded. "Except I think she actually got the Barnes' legal gene. I'm a lawyer because my entire life it was simply expected of me."

"That sounds tough."

"I have no right to complain."

"That didn't exactly agree or disagree. What am I missing? Don't tell me what you really wanted to be was a doctor."

That made him laugh. "Hardly. I don't do well with the sight of blood."

"Then what?"

"Furniture."

"Excuse me?" Those captivating blue eyes popped open wide again.

"As a kid, Pops, my mother's dad, taught me how to whittle. Soon after mastering how to make a whistle from a small piece of driftwood, I advanced to stepstools, small bookcases, and side tables."

Her head bobbed and he could feel those eyes seeing right through him. "You still love it."

"Yeah. I do."

To her credit, she waited what felt like a long time for him to offer more information before she spoke up again. "You're good at it too."

None of these were questions, but he nodded anyhow.

"And I'm guessing you graduated from small step stools."

Again, he nodded.

"Are we going to play twenty questions all night?" The soft smile on her lips, cushioned the harshness of her words.

"I can pretty much make anything a person could want, but ever since making my first rocking chair for my grandmother, that's the item most frequently requested by their friends."

"So you're a lawyer who makes furniture on the side."

"Not so much on the side, more like every once in a while. If work gets exceptionally critical or stressful, I can think more clearly after a short while of working with my hands."

"Which is why you knew to better brace the dresser we assembled."

"Pretty much." He nodded again. "I would have rather made one from scratch."

"I bet it would have been lovely." Her gaze took on an almost dreamy look, but he saw nothing but sincerity in her eyes.

"Thank you."

"Have you ever thought about giving up the law to make furniture? There is such a lack of quality nowadays that for every ten people who want cheap and easy DIY furniture, there's at least one or two willing to pay for a solid American-made piece that they can pass down for generations."

"More than once, but I'm afraid it would destroy my father."

"Can't your sister go work for the family firm? She is a lawyer."

"She already does."

Jo blinked hard, then frowned. "So where's the problem?"

"She's not his son."

"So?"

So. Such a simple word. He ran it around in his head. Why did he have to remain in the firm when his sister so clearly loved her job more than he ever would?

Jo continued, "Maybe, because my father never had sons, it never occurred to him to treat us any differently. Though I'm not sure he intended for his kids to take over the family business. He's always said when he retires, he'd sell and take Mom everywhere she'd ever wanted to go."

"What is the family business?"

"We own an Italian delicatessen."

"Your dad started it?"

"With his brother. All us kids, my sisters and me and my cousins, worked the store at some point or other when we were teens, but none of us showed any interest in making it our careers. I guess I never really thought about it."

"And there's the difference. We've got over a hundred years of precedent. Dad grew up expecting to be a lawyer, and expecting to have sons who would be lawyers too."

"I guess expectations can be a pain."

"Not the word that came to my mind, but yeah." Which made his mind wander in a different direction. "What if we don't win this? If there's no prize money to take home? How will you feel?"

"Like I've made a fool of myself on national television?" Again, her smile softened the delivery of her words. "I could ask you the same thing."

"I think I'd feel worse for Colleen. She's one of those people who live paycheck to paycheck. She's not starving by any means, but she's always playing the lottery in hopes of finally having enough money for a down payment on a little house."

Jo's smile brightened. "Then I guess we can't lose. How's your sand castle-building skills?"

He really wished she hadn't reminded him of tomorrow's challenge. What he was discovering to be a pattern, the powers that be hadn't shared exactly what tomorrow's challenge would entail, but the words castles in the sand were tossed around more than once. And this city boy had spent very little time near any water apart from the bathtub. "Lacking. You?"

"I'm not sure if burying my father in the sand at a trip to the beach when I was seven counts, but I'm ready to try."

That's one thing he was really learning to like about her. So many women he'd grown up with, or even dated, or worked with, would have run from the room screaming at the first unexpected activity.

Ginnie came up to Jo's side. "I think it's time to cut the happy girls over there off. We're heading back to the cabin. Coming with us?"

"Yeah. Tomorrow's an early start. I'll follow you." Her sister turned away and Jo leaned in, closing the distance between them, and gave him a quick peck on the cheek, followed by a fast "don't stay up too late. Tomorrow starts early." And then she was gone.

It took all his years of experience not letting the other side see what you really think, to keep from putting his hand on his cheek and feel the remaining sizzle from the lightest of touches. If this is how he felt after only a couple of nights of learning to be friends, he might be in way more trouble than he ever thought possible.

CHAPTER TEN

Breakfast had gone pretty much the same as it had the day before, except today, Mina and Brenda remained in bed sound asleep. Jo supposed if you have a right to stay in bed, it has to be while on vacation.

Apparently, a morning meeting of the teams was a one-time thing. In order for Carson and Dylan to spend some time together, Carson had arranged to spend equal time with all the contestants. There was no room for favorites. They had pretty much skirted the whole "friend with the producer" issue by a technicality, if the show was to succeed for several seasons, if not years, the way Carson hoped, whoever won had to win fair and square. And that was Jo and Dylan's plan.

"I have to admit. You two are looking good."

Jo wasn't sure if thank you was in order or not.

"What's the story with Jay and Sandy?" Dylan asked what Jo had been wondering.

"First of all, if I knew, I wouldn't be able to tell you. But there's no rule against fraternizing with the teams, you're welcome to ask them yourselves."

"So you don't know?" Dylan pushed.

"Honestly, I don't know anything about anyone except you." His head turned to face Jo. "And I know nothing about you other than you're not Colleen." His gaze shifted back to his childhood friend. "As you know, I came in on this very last minute. I haven't even had time to read the notes I was given on the selection process. My concern has been on moving forward, and watching the daily rushes to make sure we have enough interesting material to keep the television viewing audience awake."

"Oh, please tell me there won't be staged catastrophes and fights. I hate those." She really did. Whether on a TV show or a movie or a book. Forced drama drove her nuts.

"Not if the show is organically interesting enough." Carson flashed a toothy smile that might as well have shouted *please do something interesting*. "Not that we want anything like the guest star on a dance show passing out on camera."

"I thought you said we're not live." Dylan frowned at his friend.

Carson nodded. "Correct, but, originally the whole thing was going to be live. Then we thought just the first episode which would give us a week for editing the next episode. But in the end, it was decided that the show needed more of a marketing push and everything got quietly pushed back a week to all taped shows. No one will be seeing our first furniture building effort for a while."

"I guess it didn't hurt that Colin and Debbie fell flat on their derrieres?" Jo bit back a smile.

"Or that Sandy was almost on the verge of tears. Viewers love human interest. Oh," Carson snapped his fingers, "I forgot to tell you. There's going to be an interview segment so you guys need to figure out your shtick."

"Our what?" the two echoed.

"How you decided to find romance online, first interaction, why you fell in love, you know, the human interest side."

"Carson," Dylan sighed, "I don't think how we met on the first day of the cruise over a sick fake girlfriend is going to do your ratings any good."

"How many times do I have to tell you? Don't let the word reality fool you. Massage the truth." Carson waved at Dylan. "After the online speed dating, you couldn't forget Jo's smile or Jo couldn't forget yours. Things like that. Take a bit of truth and spin it. You're a lawyer, spin should come naturally."

Though he didn't know it, Carson had a point. Once she'd finally noticed Dylan, he was somewhat difficult to forget. And the more she spoke with him, the more intrigued she'd become. He was different from most of the guys she hung out with or had dated. She couldn't quite put her finger on it, but something drew her into wanting to put all the pieces together that was Dylan Barnes. Like trying to assemble a jigsaw puzzle when you'd lost the only image of what the outcome should be.

"My time is up." Carson pushed to his feet. "Have to meet the crew on the beach. I'll catch you for a drink or something later."

Both of them nodded at the man as he hurried away from the table.

"Do you think he knows more than he's sharing with us?" Her gaze remained on the associate producer's disappearing back.

"Yes and no."

She let out a sharp laugh that sounded more like a small dog. "Gotta love a straight to the point answer."

That brought a smile to his face. "Sorry. What I meant is that I'm sure there are things he knows about the show that he's not sharing, nor will he share. On the other hand, I don't think he'd deliberately lie to me."

"How about massage the truth?" She cocked her head sideways at him.

Dylan waved his hand from side to side in a maybe yes, maybe no gesture. "Only time will tell."

"Speaking of time." She pushed away from the table. "I want to check in with the girls before we head to the beach. Make sure Mina and Brenda woke up without their heads rolling off their shoulders."

"They didn't drink that much."

"Maybe not for you, but from what I've heard, all it took for those two to be dancing on a table top in New Orleans was one Hurricane. Of course, Ginnie hadn't been there to keep them in line. Anyhow, I want to find out where they'll be when we're done."

"Sounds like a plan. I might check in with the office. See how Cassie is doing keeping Dad from stressing himself into a heart attack."

"Is he ill?"

Dylan shook his head. "No, but if he doesn't slow down, he will be. All of us, including Mom, try to rein Dad in."

"Okay. Let me know how they're all doing."

"Will do."

Like she'd done last night, she leaned over and kissed him on the cheek. It had been such a force of habit thing to do last night. After all, she was Italian, kissing people hello and goodbye was as normal as putting milk in cereal, but after she'd pulled back, turned away, and realized what she'd done, the gesture had gone from daily habit to feeling very natural. Now, while she walked away, the feeling fluttering in her gut had shifted from natural to right. And wasn't that something she hadn't expected?

At least this time the quick peck on the cheek hadn't caught him quite so off guard. What had caught him by surprise was the unexpected hope that next time she'd shift a little closer to his mouth.

Shaking that thought loose, he reminded himself this was all just a game, a pretense. When the filming was over, they'd go back to their friends and family and homes far away. Homes. Good grief. He had no idea where home was for her. Wouldn't that be one of the first things a real couple would know? Where were you born, where do you live, what's your favorite color? No, he nixed that. Pretty much every counseling or newlywed show on television proved that most couples had no idea about the others' favorite color, flower, or food. Still, next chance they had, it might be prudent to go over a list of questions. No reason not to approach this like any other case. No lawyer goes into court and asks questions he doesn't already know the answer to.

Pulling out his phone, he hit his sister's number. In a matter of seconds, her voice boomed through the speaker. "You pick one hell of a time to go off on a boys' vacation."

Uh-oh. "Things are going that well, are they?"

"I swear, some days I want to walk away and start a firm with nothing but women and take on only female clients. Tell me why it is that women clients have no trouble dealing with you men, but unless we have a third appendage below the waist, the good old boys club just can't see us."

"What did he do?"

"You mean that chauvinistic, pompous—"

"Watch it. Big brother—or Dad—may be listening."

"He's having lunch with the pompous ... potential client."

"I'll only be gone eight more days. Can't Dad stall?"

The dead silence on the other end of the phone told Dylan all he needed to know. His sister wasn't considering his words, she was staring daggers at the phone.

"I can't see you."

"No. If we could have stalled, don't you think we would have tried that before you took off on your sunny beachside vacation?"

"Point taken." The single word Jo had tossed at him last night *so* had him rethinking the way he dealt with his sister. After their dad, she was the best attorney at the firm. It was time he stopped treating her like a kid sister and more like the stellar lawyer she was. "What do you suggest I do?" Another short moment of silence and he hoped his sister was contemplating the question, not shooting death rays at him.

"Let me think on it. Keep your phone handy."

"Will do my best. Whatever you need, I'm here for you." He hoped she'd always known that. It had never occurred to him that he'd never told his sister.

"I know." The way her voice softened, he knew she meant it. At least he hadn't let her down that much. "I have to run. I think they're back. Do your best to have a good time. I'm on this."

It occurred to him that it would be best if he and Jo arrived at their beach destination together, so he shot her a quick text and agreed upon a time and place to meet. Off the ship, the designated beach was within walking distance.

Halfway there, he extended his hand and latched on to hers. "Appearances," he reminded her. He doubted he'd needed to remind her; after all, it was originally her idea to begin with.

To his surprise, over the entry to the beach, a huge banner hung announcing the show.

"Nothing like subtlety," Jo muttered.

"Look at all that." Sandy came to a stop behind them. It was probably the first time he'd noticed her speak besides softly calling out answers for the dance relay. He also noticed she seemed to be standing a bit closer to Jay than usual. Whether or not that meant anything, he didn't have a clue.

Laid out in three separate sections were hundreds of sand castles. Some large, some small, and just about every size in between.

"There are fifty per section," the security guard to one side offered.

"What are we going to do with fifty sand castles?" Colin and his other half now stood to Dylan's other side. He was afraid to ask that question out loud.

"Welcome, ladies and gentlemen," the host's voice boomed through a hand-held megaphone. After doing the expected promotional speech for the new show, he proceeded to explain the rules of the new game. "Hidden in one of your fifty sand castles is a note with a clue to where your onshore lunch date will be. But there's a catch."

Something told Dylan he wasn't going to like this, but if he had to back in the hot sand like King Tut in his sarcophagus, it might be enough for him to pay Jo and Colleen their shares out of his 401k, take the hit, and call the whole thing a learning lesson.

"Once you have found the note, you will have to rebuild the destroyed castle."

Debbie's jaw dropped and for the first time in three days, Dylan was pretty sure Colin finally lost the cocky smile.

"Of course, no one expects you to create an exact replica, but you'll have all the materials necessary to create something of similar size and appearance. Once the judges approve, you'll be able to head out for your lunch date." The guy took his time reading the audience and a sly smile came across his face. "And there's one more little something I forgot to mention about the note. It won't show you the name of the location, but a riddle. First couple to their final destination will get the most points."

Just what Dylan needed. He hated riddles. And either the look on his face or the sound of his breath heavily exhaling must have tipped Jo off. Her hand pulled loose from his and she gently patted the small of his back. Was her reassuring gesture just a coincidence, another example of a good heart? Or could she read him so well all ready?

CHAPTER ELEVEN

"I give up." Jo stood with her hands on her hips while Dylan tapped at his phone. Some days men drove her nuts. What the heck could be more important than digging in and finding the dumb note. "There's a time limit on this sucker and the others are already attacking their first castle."

"I know." Dylan pointed at the sandy castle in front of him and clicked. "This way if the note is there, we know what we're rebuilding."

Jo grinned wide and had to resist the urge to lean over and kiss him. "I knew there was a reason I liked you."

"You like me?" A teasing grin crossed his lips before he returned his attention to the castle. "Since we have no idea how small the paper is—I mean it could be as tiny as a fortune in a cookie—we should sift through the castle more like an archeologist approaching a ruin."

"Good idea. Besides, the less we destroy, the less we have to rebuild."

"Exactly." He grinned at her again. "I knew there was a reason I liked you."

Rather than repeat what he'd said before, she rolled her eyes and wetting her hands in a nearby bucket of water, she grabbed a handful of soft sand, molded it quickly into a ball and tossed it at him.

"Hey!" He toppled back on his haunches and she swore she saw his nostrils flare like a bull about to charge the idiot who trespassed on his pasture.

Oops. "Remember. Note to find." Just in case, she plastered on a toothy grin and scooted back a few inches.

"You are so lucky we have a job to do."

Again, she had to resist the urge to lean over and kiss him. But as she'd said before, they had a job to do. They'd made it through five castles when Colin sprang up, giving a cheer. Dylan had been right about the size of paper. It was indeed small. Not as small as a fortune cookie, but not as big as a Post-It either. Had they simply tore the sand castles apart they might have buried the paper in a handful of sand without ever noticing it at all.

"Keep focused," Dylan said so softly she almost didn't hear him.

It took a short second for her to realize she'd been staring at the couple who were frowning at the piece of paper held between them. Finding the paper was only one of three steps. Dylan was right. If they wanted to win, she had to keep focused. "Sorry," she whispered back.

Wiping sweat away from his brow with the back of his arm, he shot her a smile and went back to work. Colin and Debbie had stopped staring at the paper and turned to rebuilding the sand castle. From their still narrowed gazes, Jo would bet they had no idea what the clue meant.

Two sandcastles later, Colin and Debbie were still working on rebuilding. Apparently, one or the other hadn't mastered the mixture of sand and water to keep the thing from crumbling away. From the way Debbie kept talking through a plastered on plastic smile, Jo had a feeling there was nothing lovey-dovey being said now. Jo dared glance over at Jay and Sandy. At least they were talking to each other this time. The pair were too far away for Jo to hear, but Jay seemed to be doing most of the talking. Actually, now that Jo watched them for a few minutes, she got the feeling he was cheering her on. She couldn't help but think how sweet they looked working together. Out here in the sun, the two looked so young.

"Look." Dylan pointed in front of her hands.

So intent on watching the others, she'd almost missed it. The note. "We found it!" The urge to lean forward and kiss him was too strong to resist. Leaning left, she lifted her chin to reach his cheek, not expecting him to turn and speak at that exact moment. Instead of his cheek, her lips landed smack dab against his.

All the breath in her lungs seemed to whoosh out like a deflated balloon. The unexpected was short and sweet and she couldn't bring herself to pull fully away. "I, uh, we … found the note."

Not moving, he bobbed his head. "Yeah."

She hadn't expected the simple touch of lips to shoot waves of rolling heat all the way to her toes. Or maybe it was the tropical sun? Or maybe Dylan was quickly becoming more than a means to an end?

All Dylan had meant to do was ask Jo to read the riddle. He hadn't realized she was leaning in for one of her quick pecks on the cheek. When her lips pressed against his, he'd come within inches of pulling her closer and kissing her for real, and yet, that all too short contact had impacted him more than any intentional kiss since his first awkward kiss in junior high.

"I guess I should read it?"

All he could do was nod.

"Liberty is essential but the true meaning of the bell is for all eternity." Her forehead crumpled into deep creases and the startled glint in her eyes disappeared. "What the heck?"

Since they were visitors unfamiliar with the island, the production crew had given them a list of every restaurant, café, and bar. And there were way more than he'd expect to find in a big city, never mind a small island. "Is there anything on the list that has something to do with liberty or freedom?"

Her gaze dropped to the page as she muttered, "I suppose it would be asking too much to find a Liberty Bell Bar and Grill on the list."

He held back a chuckle. "I would think so."

"No liberty or freedom. Not even a bell."

Nothing jumped out at him as having anything to do

with liberty, bells, or eternity, but the answer had to be there somewhere. "Let's try eternity. What are other words for eternity? Infinity, forever, endless, heaven—"

"Wait a minute."

He was really learning to love the way her eyes lit up when she got enthused over some little thing.

"The meaning of the bell. Maybe it's not liberty or eternity, but the bell. Look." She held the paper in front of him and pointed to one name. It took him a few seconds to make the connection, but then he nodded.

Her smile as wide as the island they were about to cross, their words tumbled over each other. "Every time a bell rings, an angel gets his wings." He almost asked how many times she's seen the old movie "It's a Wonderful Life" but now wasn't the time to explore his love for classic films.

"The Angel Wings Café it is." The way she bounced in place, for just a split second, he thought she was going to lean over and kiss him again. Instead her finger waved in his direction. "Where's the castle photo? We have places to go."

Thankfully, they'd not destroyed the lower half of the castle, but the paper had been buried far enough inside that they had some work to do.

"What's your sand castle experience?" she asked him, holding an empty bucket in her hand.

Dylan shrugged. "So so. And you?"

"That sounds better than me."

He'd been hoping for a more resounding history of sand sculptures, but he supposed a confession of awful could have been worse.

"How about I run and get the water and I'll let you deal with the construction?"

Reluctantly, he nodded. "Not sure that I'll be any better than you, but it's a start. I'll begin working with the dry sand."

She nodded as though she had every confidence in the world that he knew what he was doing. He only hoped she was right. A few short minutes later, she'd run back to their spot with a bucket of water in each hand. "What's the plan?"

Right now a career as a beach bum might have come in handier than a law degree, but he did his best. So far he'd organized the turret shaped buckets to align somewhat with the way the castle had been before demolition. "Let me have a little water. You fill that bucket with sand."

Her gaze followed the direction of his finger. With a quick nod, she did as instructed. When she paused to look up, he knew what she was watching. Colin and Debbie hurried to the curb. "Is it awful of me to hope that they screwed up and wind up at the wrong place? Because it looks like they're on their way to winning this round."

Considering he felt the same way, all he could do was nod and redirect her attention. Leaning back on his haunches, he examined the first turret. Better than he'd expected. "How's that?"

The sparkle returned to her eyes and that sweet smile reappeared. "Perfect. Maybe we can still beat Colin and Debbie."

Dylan bobbed his head and discreetly pointed to the curb ahead. "I don't think they've figured out the clue yet."

From the way the two stood at the edge of the street, that plastic smile still firmly in place for the benefit of the camera as they both waved their arms, pointing in different directions, they looked nothing like the smoldering couple on day one. They also didn't look like they could agree on a plan.

As he removed the final bucket revealing the last replaced turret, Jo waved the judges over. They too had taken photos of all the castles. Theirs wasn't identical, but as his mom used to say, *it was close enough for government work.* Jo rocked back on her heels, and at the same moment the judge nodded her approval, Sandy jumped up shouting and grinning at Jay. They'd found the paper in the very top turret. Their castle had hardly been damaged.

Something about those two made him smile. Unlike the others, Dylan was almost rooting for these guys to get it right. Maybe it was the same instinct that had a man looking out for damsels in distress and kittens stuck in trees. Whatever it was, it would have to wait. They had a café to visit. Pushing to his feet, he grabbed hold of Jo's hand and they traipsed across the hot sand, almost tripping a few times and laughing like loons. He couldn't have asked for a more perfect partner if he'd spent an entire month considering personality pros and cons.

A shout from the crowd caught his attention. Jo's sisters and friends were jumping and whistling and waving their arms. They looked happier about all this than even he and Jo did. "Were they here the whole time?"

"Who?" Jo's gaze followed the direction he was looking in.

He knew the moment she spotted her family. Her smile spread and her step lightened.

"Probably," she whispered and waved back.

When they reached the curb, Colin and Debbie were gone, but he felt in his bones they could still pull this off. A short cab ride, a brief struggle with the language barrier, and a challenging effort at paying the driver later, they hurried into the café.

In front of them a small table with two chairs had been set up. A tent card with the words *Love on Deck* worked as a centerpiece. But best of all, a group of people consisting of production crew, passengers he'd recognized as following the show, and a couple of ship's officers, stood behind the table and shouted, "Surprise!" followed by one of the production people explaining, "You're the first to complete the full challenge!"

"We did it!" So excited, Jo spun around and threw her arms around him.

Encircling his arms around her, he nodded. Only this time he leaned down and whispered, "Yes, we did," seconds before his lips came down on hers. Not by chance, not by mistake, and certainly not for show.

CHAPTER TWELVE

Three days and nights had come and gone since that one toe tingling kiss. Jo had been caught up in the whirlwind excitement of the day and the big points win when she'd thrown her arms around him in a victory hug.

At the café, she'd been delighted to learn when Jay and Sandy appeared that they had come in second in the challenge. It was also surprising as all heck to discover that Colin and Debbie had gone to three different restaurants and never successfully figured out their clue. According to comments she'd heard from the audio crew, behind the plastic smile, Debbie's words had been unfit for a family television show. Apparently, there were not three different restaurants, but all three had been given the same clue. Only Jay and Sandy had successfully solved all parts of the equation and joined them at the little café in time for a feast put on by the locals and worthy of a king's court.

As the days moved on, she realized that as with the sand castles and furniture building, all the challenges would be identical, giving each couple the same odds of success. Or failure.

The three couples had toggled back and forth on the leader board with the top spot more often than not changing places between Dylan and her, and Colin and Debbie. After the sand castle failure, their lovey-dovey cooing had been fewer and farther between. Today was the first day they'd been given both the morning and early afternoon off to visit the port on their own. Something all the girls were thrilled to get to do together. Of course they still had the cameraman following at a distance, but not only had she and Dylan become used to the conspicuously not so discreet shadow, but so had her sisters and friends. Sometimes, she was so used to them that she'd almost forget they were there. With all of them, including Dylan and Carson and poor Colleen who only felt human on dry land, doing a self-guided tour of the old city, she had indeed forgotten that they weren't ordinary tourists but characters from a television show. Sort of.

What she hadn't been able to forget was the zing that ricocheted through her as the warmth of his lips pressed against hers, or the lonely ache that took its place when the gathering of enthusiastic fans drew them apart, bathing them in praise and excitement for the new show. Even now, three days later, whenever his arm lightly brushed against hers, or his hand squeezed around her fingers, or his smiling eyes locked on hers, any brief connection had her floating back to the little café, leaving nerve ends tingling again. With only a few days left to the cruise, that lonesome ache was rearing its ugly head more and more often, and there really wasn't a dang thing she could do about it.

"Am I the only one whose feet hurt?" Jo sat down on a nearby bench, easing one shoe of her left foot then twisting to remove the other. Extending her legs straight out in front of her, she wiggled her toes. "I think we've walked all over the island and back. Twice."

Mina flopped onto the seat beside her. "You sure it wasn't three times?"

"For sure there isn't a nook or cranny of this old town we have seen." Ginnie moved to the neighboring bench and sat beside Teresa.

Teresa bobbed her head, gesturing for Brenda to squeeze onto the bench with them. "Definitely every nook and a few crannies more than once."

Craning her head from side to side, Mina frowned. "Where are Dylan and Carson?"

"They stopped to buy a souvenir for their moms, but I really wanted to sit and didn't think the shopkeeper would appreciate me doing it in the middle of her floor."

"For their moms?" Brenda leaned forward. "Is Carson still single?"

Jo nodded.

"Does he live with his mother?"

"I don't think so." Jo shook her head.

"Does he wet the bed?"

Through one narrow eye, Jo glanced at her sister's maid of honor. "How should I know, but I doubt it."

Brenda dipped her chin and smiling leaned back. "The way a man treats his mother is often a sign of how he'll treat a wife. I like thoughtful single men as long as they don't still live with their mothers." She suddenly shot forward in the seat. "Is he gay?"

Considering every chance Carson had, he'd been hitting on a well-developed blonde traveling solo, that question she had the answer to. "Nope."

Smiling, Brenda leaned back again. "I need to pay more attention since Dylan is taken."

"He is?" This time Jo shot forward.

Shaking her head, cousin Teresa started to chuckle. "She means by you."

"Me?" Had her sisters forgotten this whole arrangement was only for show?

"Yes, you," Mina chimed in. "Wait till you see the show. If you two don't win, it will be a shocker."

"I think you guys are confusing acting and love." Jo waved a thumb at Colleen standing with her face to the sun. "You tell them."

"Me?" Colleen shook her head. "What do I know? All I see onboard is the ceiling of my cabin."

Jo really did feel badly for the poor woman. No amount of meds, patches, or wrist bands made her comfortable on her feet. Just keeping her stomach calm long enough to get off the ship required moving her from the cabin to the dock in a wheelchair.

"We're not confusing anything." Shaking her head, Teresa huffed. "Next time you're looking into those stormy eyes, pay attention."

That made her frown. *Stormy*? She'd been so focused on his lips and wishing he'd kiss her again, that she hadn't noticed anything stormy about his eyes. Though it was hard to miss the way they glistened when he smiled. And of course, the caramel flecks in those chocolaty irises.

"See?" Brenda waved a tired arm at her. "She's getting that dreamy look on her face again. Probably thinking about doing the tango. If you know what I mean."

"Am not." She probably spat that out with more force than necessary.

"Speaking of which." Her cousin Teresa turned to look at her. "How are those lessons going? They won't let any passengers in to watch."

Too bad they let the cameramen in. She blew out a sigh. So far, they'd been paired off with one of the pros to learn the routine. This evening after dinner would be their first lesson dancing with each other. Considering how often she tripped over or stepped on her instructor, she was not looking forward to the session. "Coming along."

"Sounds rough." Mina frowned. "You're a pretty good dancer. Does he have two left feet?"

He wasn't the problem. "The tango is different. The rhythm is different." Hell, she'd have rather done a good old-fashioned jitterbug any day of the week.

"You two will work it out." Ginnie smiled at her, the same way she had after spending hours helping Jo with her geometry homework. And of course, her sister had been right. By the end of her sophomore year of high school, she'd become a whiz at doing proofs.

"Hey, I don't want to miss the napkin folding on board." Mina sprang to her feet as though she hadn't walked an inch all day. "Who's coming back with me?"

Everyone except her stood as Dylan and Carson strolled up to them.

"Heading back to the ship, or more sightseeing?" Carson asked.

"Ship," five voices echoed.

"Good." Carson sighed. "I'll come with you ladies. We have the afternoon challenge soon." He turned to Dylan. "Remember, four o'clock sharp."

Dylan nodded at his friend and then looked to Jo. "Ready?"

"Thought I'd rest the tootsies a few more minutes." She held up her feet and wiggled her toes again. "If you want to go ahead with Carson, I can make it back on my own."

Instead of answering yes or no, Dylan squatted down on his haunches and picked up one foot. Dang, especially down on one knee, this guy really looked like Prince Charming. Where was a girl's fairy godmother when she needed one?

Even Jo's feet were pretty. The pale pink background painted on with a tiny daisy on each big toe fit everything about her. Practical and traditional with a bit of whimsy. Carefully pushing his thumb along the edges of her heel, he watched her eyes drift shut.

"You should have skipped law and been a masseuse."

"Dad would have loved that." He found a pressure point and held it.

"Ooh." She stiffened a moment and then relaxed. "Oh, that feels better."

"That's the idea."

"I take back the masseuse comment. A foot spa." She smiled as he let her foot fall to the ground and reached for the other. "Definitely a foot spa."

"If the law falls through, I'll keep that in mind." Carefully rubbing the ball of each toe, he took in her relaxed smile.

Her head tipped to the side. "Would it really be that bad to tell your dad you'd rather not practice law? My mom has a friend whose son graduated from Harvard law school, not cheap, and a few years later he gave it all up to play guitar in a rock and roll band. His mom still talks to him."

"Why?" he chuckled.

"Because all any parent, any good parent, wants for their child is for them to be healthy and happy."

"You sound like the voice of experience. Something I should know?" He wiggled an eyebrow at her.

She rolled her eyes at him. "Not likely. I have a crazy

family. Lots of yelling, lots of meddling, and lots of fussing, but we all know we love each other. I know there are families not as blessed. I had a friend in high school who would never let me visit her at her house, she always wanted to be at mine. Then Dad thought it too late for her to walk home alone one night and he took her. He took one look at her mother when she answered the door and almost dragged her mother out of the house and kept them at our house until she could get proper help. Even found her a job at my Uncle Tony's pizza parlor."

"What happened to the father?"

Jo sighed. "I don't honestly know, but I suspect Dad knew some people, who knew some people, who didn't like a man beating up his wife any more than Dad did."

"They, uh…"

"Killed him? No. I saw him around town from time to time. He always grunted under his breath like he was trying not to growl at me."

"I'm sorry."

She shrugged. "Life isn't pretty for everyone, but my point is, the good parents care about their children. I'm betting your father will care more about your happiness than the law firm."

"I don't know about that."

"You think I'm being all Pollyanna, don't you?"

Gently, he set her foot on the ground and shrugged. "You don't understand how important the firm and its history is to Dad. He's proud of them both."

"And of you?" She slipped one foot slowly into her sandal.

He couldn't argue with that. He was very proud of his son, the junior partner.

"I don't mean you, the lawyer. I mean you, the boy who became a man. I see all the good in you, the thoughtful in you, the caring you, the gentleman, the—"

"Okay. Thank you, I think. Still…"

"I don't believe you would have become the very good man you are without a caring father. My money is on your dad understanding."

He didn't know whether to puff out his chest and shout to the world she thought he was not just a good man, but a very good man, or believe she could be right and he could walk away from the law without breaking his father's heart. Why was it that when he was with Jo, anything seemed possible? And good.

CHAPTER THIRTEEN

The entire walk back to the ship, neither said a word. Somehow, she knew he needed time to process his next step. Halfway back, he reached over and took her hand. There was something almost possessive about his hold on her, and much to her surprise, she liked it. A lot. Maybe even more than the kiss.

At the ship, they showed their cards and had barely exited the elevator when Carson came up to them. "Hey, what took you two so long? Don't either of you wear watches?"

Dylan flipped his wrist and rolled his eyes. "I forgot that island time is an hour behind ship time."

"And the call sheet is on ship's time," Jo muttered, only now realizing how slowly they'd strolled back to their floating hotel. They were now a full fifteen minutes late.

"Don't just stand there. Everyone's been waiting." Carson turned and briskly walked across the ship, passed the carefree passengers, holding the glass elevator for them.

The lounge room was already filled with passengers who had grown to enjoy the daily challenges combined with news of the day. As expected, the participants sat in separate sections, their two seats empty, waiting for them.

Briskly, they hurried to their seats, waving at her sisters as they scurried past.

"Welcome to another day of *Love on Deck*," Dirk Simpson announced with that plastic grin they'd become so used to. "I'd like to start the day off with some good news."

The anticipation in the room grew palpably stronger.

"Our editing team at home has made wonderful progress. The network is delighted with the results and have decided that our first episode will be broadcast one week early."

Gasps of surprise laced with delight filtered through the large social area.

"The first episode of *Love on Deck* will be shown live on the outdoor screen for you romantics and in the theater for those of you wusses who prefer the comfort of air conditioning."

That garnered a few chuckles throughout the audience. Debating in her own mind as to whether or not the man had ad libbed the wuss comment, what he'd said suddenly struck her. Live from the ship. Which meant none of them would be home to keep their mother from watching or at least explaining before the silly show aired.

A sense of panic rushed up her spine as she turned in search of her sisters. Both Mina and Ginnie as well as the other members of her group had grown impossibly pale. They all understood what this new glitch to their plan meant.

In the background, Dirk explained the brief challenge before dinner break. The words floated in the distance as she batted around ideas of how to keep her mother away from the TV. She paused to calculate one week early and was horrified to realize the first episode would be airing tomorrow night.

The audio guy couldn't mic her fast enough. She had only a few minutes while everyone else's mics were put in place to reach her sisters. Hopefully, one of them had already come up with a plan. If not, six heads had to be better than one.

As she stood in place, waiting for the tech guy with fumbling fingers to wire her up, Dylan reached over and took her hand. He gave it a tight squeeze. The single gesture said everything he couldn't say within microphone distance. They had a problem. From the tidbits he'd told her about his work situation, she knew that he didn't think appearing on a reality game show would be good for business. As a matter of fact, he was concerned that it could down right hurt his company's chances of succeeding. He'd expected to be home to seal a deal before the show aired. Now that opportunity was taken away from him, and he knew full well that this was all going to come as a shocking surprise to her mother.

Another squeeze accompanied by an unconvincing smile told her what she already knew deep in her gut. Whatever happened, he'd be there for her. And that did more to calm her rising panic than a bottle of tequila and an emergency flight home.

Glancing up to where her sisters sat, she noticed Mina with a phone to her ear, moving her hands faster than an orchestra conductor waving his baton. With Ginnie here there was only one person Jo could think of that her sister would call. It had to be Kent.

Watching her oldest sister as the audio tech moved to Dylan, she actually saw her sister's shoulders deflate and a soft smile push away the worried expression. A slight movement of Mina's shoulder and a dip of her head and it became clear that she was indeed talking to her fiancé. Even at a crazy time like this, her sister looked so happy.

Jo was thrilled with how much Mina and Kent loved each other. The way they each lit up when the other walked into a room. The sweet smiles that accompanied soft words meant only for each other. There was no doubt in Jo's mind that those two would make it the distance, and happily, the same as their parents. She, on the other hand, had more to do and explore before being tied down. And then, as the old seventies' song said, she planned to shop around before settling down. At least, that's what she'd thought.

As if he was reading her mind, Dylan offered a soft smile and once more, squeezed her hand. Suddenly, right now, she didn't want to shop around, and couldn't imagine exploring places and things with anyone but Dylan. What she really wanted was to walk hand in hand with this man for the rest of her days. So now that left the question; what was she going to do about it?

Because of the late time of day, everyone expected today's challenge to be short and sweet. The second Dylan and Jo were handed large thick straws, he knew he'd rather assemble do-it-yourself cheap furniture.

"All right," Dirk announced. "Today's challenge is simple. You'll notice our staff are setting up three rows of paper plates on cocktail tables. There is a piece of candy on the first plate."

Their host didn't need to say another word for Dylan to know where this was going. No doubt, whatever the task, they'd probably look ridiculous on TV, but he could see where the viewership would eat it up. It hadn't taken him long to figure out, the sillier the stunt, or the more contentious the relationship issues, the higher the expected ratings. So far, more than once, a camera had descended on a couple outside of the call sheet schedule. Obviously, one of the production crew spotted something that would spice up the show, and like moths to a flame, they'd all appeared to capture the moment.

"The idea," Dirk continued, "is to suck up the candy and take it to the next plate. Hands behind your back, you'll each take turns from plate to plate. First couple to the end wins the points for the day."

Oh, this was not going to be pretty. Rushing simultaneously, there were the expected drops and starting overs, the one party bumping into the other and laughing or shouting or even looking tearful, the audience cheering and soaking it all up, and in the end, Jay and Sandy won, moving them up to second place. It had taken a while, but they finally had begun to look each other in the eye and even stand close enough to touch. Jo had said it more than once and he was beginning to believe she was right. They were a cute couple. Young, a little scared, but cute. Debbie looked less than happy to not have won, but no amount of sweet talking from Colin could change her mood. There was definitely at least a little trouble in that paradise.

As for Dylan, he didn't really care who had won, all he wanted was to get this mic off and find someplace private to talk to Jo. Another few minutes and they were both free and trotting over to where her sisters had been waiting.

"Any ideas?" Jo looked to her siblings.

No one looked terribly enthused, but Mina took the lead. "Kent has an idea or two. We're to call him back when you're free and nail it down."

Jo nodded, but didn't look convinced.

"I need to call my sister," Dylan said. A lot of money and sweat had gone into garnering this feather in the firm's cap. If they lost this opportunity to win over the Costa Brewery as a new client because of this ridiculous television idea, he wouldn't have to worry about telling his father he wanted to leave. The firm would toss him out on his briefcase.

Before he could step aside and pull out his phone, the thing sounded off loudly. A quick glance at the name and he waved a finger at Jo to let her know he'd be right back, and walked away from the gathering, away from the cameramen, and away from prying eyes. "Hey, Sis."

"Don't you hey Sis me. What the hell were you thinking?"

Surely she hadn't heard he was on the show already? Or had the network begun advertising using film clips?

"You should know better than to think telling a woman not to tell her best friend something important would work." She sounded like an angry mom scolding her three-year-old.

"Mom knows?" It wasn't really a question.

"That *you* are on the reality show? Of course she does. Have you lost your ever-loving mind?"

He'd asked himself that more than once when this all started. "Actually—"

"Do you realize what this will do to our chances of landing any new accounts, never mind the one Dad's been chasing for half a decade."

"It shouldn't matter."

"Have you been day drinking?"

"Of course not." Though even he recognized the absurdity of his comment. If he hadn't known it would matter, he wouldn't have been in such a rush to call his sister. Who, as usual, beat him to the punch line.

"Then you are crazy. We've been doing our best with the CEO of Costa, but he's been asking for you every day. I have no idea what you did to get him to look at us, but he's not clicking with Dad."

"I gave him Mom's goulash recipe."

"Our mom?"

"Yes."

"She doesn't cook."

"I know that, and you know that, but Mr. Constantine didn't know that."

"Now I know beyond the shadow of any doubt you are not just a little crazy, you are completely off your rocker."

"It's quite simple. Remember I told you he and I met at the dinner party the Van Horns threw? Well, it was clear he not only knew his beers, but he's also a foodie, then I realized it was more than that, he was a cook. Turns out, his favorites are old Eastern European family recipes. After he critiqued the hostess's Hungarian Goulash, I told him Mom always said the secret is in the sauce. Something about extra cream, so I offered to send him Mom's old family recipe."

"Considering Mom can burn water, don't you think that was a little risky? And what do you know about making goulash?"

"*I Remember Mama.*"

"That does it. You have been day drinking. A lot."

He sighed. "It's an old black and white movie with Irene Dunn, and she mentioned the recipe. Anyhow, I knew Dad had been after this guy forever and a day. I had to do something to keep him on the hook. He gave me his private email to send the recipe. And I did."

"What recipe? Mom doesn't cook and I'm sure the movie didn't take time to broadcast a recipe."

"Of course not. Whenever there's a pot luck lunch, Karen, the receptionist at the satellite office, is always bringing delicious casseroles and such. All she ever says is 'my mother made it,' so I asked if her mother had a favorite goulash recipe. Turns out she did."

"So basically you lucked out and then decided to abandon us for a damn television show. I don't know whether to laugh or crawl through the phone and strangle you."

"It's just a television show. We simply have to couch it properly."

"That's like saying you're just a lawyer. We have a reputation for being the best of the best at practicing law, not at partying on cruise ships, or picking a mate through a television game show. Fake or not. Is it too late to change your name?"

"What?" Now he was beginning to think maybe it was his sister who had spent too much time in the hot sun.

"On the show. Not the firm. Though now that I think about it..."

"If we're lucky, most of our clients don't even watch shows like this, never mind connect me to the law firm. I'm telling you, this is no different than going into a courtroom and putting the right spin on a case for the jury. You can do that with your hands tied behind your back."

"Me? He's your new best foodie buddy. You figure this mess out and when you get off that boat, he's all yours to spin any way you want."

"Yeah, well, there's the catch."

"I don't like those words."

"The first episode is airing tomorrow, not after I get home."

A sound too similar to a low rumbling growl carried through the phone line before her heard a resigned sigh. "I'll talk to Karen see what other Eastern European recipes her mother has up her sleeve. Maybe we can keep him distracted with food for a few more days. But you need to get your backside home. Soon."

"Noted."

"Which brings me to the rest of what Carson told his mother. He says that you and your fake partner are looking pretty ... tight. Is he right?"

"Define tight." He didn't like how long his sister was taking to respond. A silent sister was never a good thing. "Cassie?"

"Holy judges. I know that tactic. Redirect and avoid.

Carson *is* right. You're falling for her."

His mouth fell open to present his arguments when he spotted Jo waving him back to the group. His heart did a quick kick and his lips pulled into a tight smile. Turning his attention back to the phone, he stared at his sister's name. Carson wasn't right at all. He wasn't falling for Jo. He'd already tumbled head over sandals for her. On a deep sigh, he waved back at Jo, then looked to the phone again. The real question he needed to answer was what the heck was he going to do about it?

CHAPTER FOURTEEN

One good thing about the tango classes were the shoes. She loved them. Buttery leather, a decent heel height for her five-foot-four stature, and leather soles that made gliding on the wooden dance floor as easy as walking on a cloud. What she wasn't thrilled about was the costume rack. She was by no means a prude, but all the dresses had slits up to her hip that made her very uncomfortable. Especially when the choreography required her to stick her leg out multiple times which, of course, showed the world all that God had given her.

"Ready?" Jorge, her instructor, gave her a broad smile.

That smile attached to a strong chiseled face, with a dimple on each cheek and piercing black eyes under long dark lashes that any woman would envy, should have had enough wattage to make her weak in the knees. Not long ago it would have, but not today. The only man's smile making her weak in the knees belonged to Dylan. Never again would she tease her sister about falling head over heels in love with a man in only a few days. She'd also have to give more credit to all those love-at-first-sight movies. Who knew it really could happen?

"Jo?" Jorge's gaze on her narrowed.

"Sorry. Yes, I'm ready." Or at least as ready as she'd ever be.

"Bravo." Natalie, Dylan's instructor, flashed a grin at her then Dylan before facing Jorge. "We will run through the routine for you once and then as you've learned all week, you will do it together. Si?"

They both bobbed their heads, but Jorge and Natalie, who happened to be married *and* from Argentina, had way more confidence in Jo's skills than she did. The dance started out slow and steady. Every so often, their foot came up behind them in a swirly motion as if kicking away the unwanted affections of an amorous mutt. That part she could do. Then Natalie's hips swiveled from left to right multiple times, seconds before one leg shot straight up in the air.

As if Jo could ever do that without unscrewing her leg first. She was sure when she did that move her leg couldn't reach more than a foot off the ground. Another second later and the same leg that had gone up to the sky came down, Natalie's foot waved behind her, and then came up onto Jorge's hip. Somehow, Natalie looked much closer to Jorge than Jo had been during their lessons. That same leg went down around and back up against Jorge a second time and Jo caught a glimpse of Dylan looking her way. She could feel the heat rising up her cheek.

The slow gliding forward and back was absolutely flawless. They looked like molten lava pouring across the floor. When Jorge took two long steps back, and Natalie's feet remained in place as her body remained a flat board leaning forward against him, Jo's breath caught. That was the one move that still terrified her every time they got to it. The feeling of falling flat on her face and breaking her nose and who knew what else, almost paralyzed her every time. Yet, Natalie made it look so easy, so beautiful.

Jo stole a glance at Dylan this time and the intensity with which he focused on their instructors made Jo wonder if that move was as much as a challenge for him as it was for her. The music and steps slowed, and next came the part where Natalie's back leg stretched far out bringing her near to the floor in an almost split. No way Jo had gone that low. Nor could she. Jorge pulled the woman slowly upright and then almost dragged her across the floor as she remained perfectly still. Somehow Jo knew she and Jorge had done something like these moves, but at the time they felt more like work. These two were fully clothed, totally silent, and raising the temperature in the room to a near boil.

Finally, a few more swirls, slides, heated meeting of

eyes, and the final move, the dip, came. Natalie's head was mere millimeters from the floor and yet she didn't flinch. They were stupendous.

"Okay," Natalie smiled, stepping away from Jorge. "Your turn."

Jo pushed to her feet and doubted even a long prayer would help. At her side, Dylan either sensed her doubts and wanted to reassure her, or perhaps needed reassurance. For whichever reason, his hand shot out and briefly clasped hers, sharing a strength of will she desperately needed. There was little doubt in her mind, one way or the other, she was going to embarrass the heck out of herself. And on national television to boot. But at least if she had to screw this up, she couldn't think of anyone she'd rather be screwed up with.

Dylan had no idea how they were going to pull off anything that looked even close to the routine they just watched. He also had no clue why the production team—including his best friend—were so eager to humiliate the contestants. Even though a loud voice in the back of his head screamed, *ratings, you moron.*

"We're going to take the first part nice and slow. Take your positions." Jorge watched as they faced each other about six inches apart. "Good. Natalie, la musica. The music."

The familiar tango tune began and Dylan closed his eyes, waiting for the music cue to move forward.

"Eyes. Eyes. Eye contact is as much a part of the dance as the steps."

Dylan's eyes sprang open. "Sorry."

Starting the music again from the beginning, Natalie waved a hand at them. Right on cue, Dylan kept his gaze leveled with Jo and took a step back. He almost stopped to cheer that he'd done it. Instead, they continued the sometimes swivel, sometimes walking step. So far, his nightmares of tripping over his own two feet and sending Jo flying across the room had not come to fruition.

The music stopped and Jorge came up beside them. "Very good. Let's try that again. This time a little closer. Neither of you has cooties." He pushed Dylan another couple of inches closer and moved his hand a tiny bit further down Jo's back.

For days, he'd been walking holding hands with Jo or nudging her along with his hand on the small of her back and nothing had happened. Why now did every nerve ending feel as though they were on fire?

As before, he followed the steps Natalie had taught him over the last few days. This time he barely missed a step, but rather than stop, he kept going.

"Good, good. Muy bien," Natalie encouraged him. "Excellent."

Instead of stopping the music at the same spot as before, they let it play until the moment he took two steps back and Jo leaned into him, her feet remaining in place the whole time. It had taken him a while with Natalie to get over the idea that if he made one wrong move, he could easily drop her flat on her face. Rather than be equally concerned about Jo's safety, instead, he couldn't get past the look in her eyes. Expecting fear, or nerves, or maybe even irritation at the evolving situation, all he saw, or thought he saw, was trust. Could it be that she really trusted him not to screw this up and drop her flat on her face?

"Very good." Jorge smiled. "Let's keep going."

Keep going. Right. Dylan moved forward and took his place in front of Jo. The music started and in perfect synchronization, they moved back. Well, he moved back and she moved forward. They kicked swiveled, and Dylan did his best not to lose his breath when Jo hiked her knee on his hip. Thank heaven when Natalie had been teaching him the routine, he'd struggled with keeping time and running his hand from her knee to her hip, so they'd cut that from the choreography. Had he had to do that now with Jo, he'd have lost his mind altogether.

By the time they'd finally made it through the entire

routine, Dylan had had about as much of this dance as any man could handle with a woman who had no idea how he felt about her. When Jorge called for one last time, Dylan almost groaned, but one more time he would do.

Natalie began the music and on cue they moved along. She had told him several times that a good tango dancer didn't think, he just moved. Like with all aspects of life, muscle memory was apparently key in the tango. Maybe it was his imagination, but he thought they were moving more fluid, easier, not having to think as hard. Was that even possible? Though in a way it made perfect sense. A beautiful woman in a man's arms, they should be able to move to their own music. A smile tugged at his lips. That idea could grow on him.

"Slow down, this is not a race." Jorge shook his head and signaled for Natalie to keep the music playing. Moving in beside them, he moved his hands like a hula dancer in slow motion. "Easy, take it easy. You are making love on the dance floor."

Dylan nearly swallowed his tongue and tripped over his own feet.

"No lover goes so fast," Jorge scolded, slowly retreating backwards to where his wife stood by the AV equipment. "Eyes. Eyes."

After that last bit of instruction, it took all the courage Dylan could muster to look Jo in the eye. There was no missing the bright pink that singed her cheeks. Dylan sucked in a deep breath, ordering his pounding heart to be still. They could do this. They had to do this. If only everything hadn't become so darn complicated.

It took every ounce of determination Jo had to get through the dance routine and ignore Jorge's romantic, if not misguided, suggestions. A towel around her neck and her bare feet stretched out before her, she had no idea how she was going to get through this again and again before the finale.

"Looking good." Carson came walking up to her. Did the man ever say anything else? "Giving you a heads up. Your interview sessions are in fifteen minutes."

"Fifteen?" She looked down at her tired feet. There was no way she could clean up and be camera ready in fifteen minutes. "I need more time."

Carson shook his head. "Nope. Since there's no filming of practice this will give the audience a feel for how hard you guys are really working. Believe it or not, sweat sells."

She didn't even want to think about it.

"Surely we can explain how hard we're working after we shower?" Dylan rubbed his sweat soaked hair with the small towel and Jo wondered if there wasn't a law against looking so sweaty and so good. Then she remembered Carson's words and almost laughed.

"No," Carson shook his head, "just the way you are. Fifteen minutes. Get your stories straight."

"Is it me," Jo kept her gaze on the man's departing back, "or is he becoming a tyrant?"

Dylan burst out laughing. "It's not you. If he keeps it up, I may have to call his mother."

"Oh." She knew she was smiling wider than she should have. "I like that idea."

"You ready for the interview?" He took a seat on the bench beside her.

"Think so. We've got it mostly worked out. I just hope I don't get nervous and forget my own name."

"Giuseppa Antonia Ummarino."

"You know my middle name?"

He shrugged. "Mina may have mentioned it."

"When did you talk to Mina about my name?"

"It wasn't about your name, it just came up when I was waiting for you one day."

Hmm. She wasn't sure if that was good or bad, and right now with sore feet and a good-looking guy at her side, she wasn't sure she cared either.

"Is everyone ready?" Dirk Simpson walked into the room with a cameraman standing behind him. For just a moment she wondered what they would all say if she'd answered, "Can I have a few more minutes to get my lies straight?"

Dirk and the cameraman told them to remain on the bench, and set up directly in front of them. "So, let's start with you, Jo."

Instantly, her back stiffened and Dylan reached over and took hold of her hand. Her gaze drifted in his direction and he could see the silent thank you in her eyes.

"What made you want to do this show?"

For a flash of an instant he could see the surprise in her eyes. Neither of them had anticipated that question, and then he saw when she settled on her reply. "For my family. My parents always put us first. Worked hard, never took trips. Our vacations were the family together on Sunday afternoons. I thought it might be nice for all of us to take a trip back to Italy. A real vacation."

Dylan had never thought to ask her that question, but her answer didn't surprise him. And he could see by the glint in Dirk's eyes, that he was counting the ratings jump.

"Family is important to you?"

Her smile brightened. "Very."

Dirk took a long minute to consider his next question. "Do you want a family of your own?"

"Some day. Yes." Her gaze shifted for such a short fraction of a moment in his direction, he wasn't sure anyone else had even noticed. "But I don't want to settle, I want a strong caring man who shares my values, my love of old movies, my sense of family, who stays calm in the sight of adversity, but who still is willing to take a chance, keep life adventurous. A partner. I don't want to split responsibilities. I want to share them."

Partner. Not till he'd been given so many tasks to do that required truly working together had he realized that even though his parents were happily married, they'd set an example of delegating responsibilities. Dad called the guy to fix the dripping faucet and Mom made the pediatrician appointments. He wanted more. He wanted a partner. Someone who believed in him. Who would encourage him to follow his dreams even if most people would consider them crazy.

His mind flashed back to how they'd solved the riddle about the Angel's wings, to her kind words for him and his dad at the park when he was rubbing her feet, to all the little conversations they'd shared between the times they were on display, and his heart pounded against his ribs wondering if he could possibly fill those shoes.

"That's a tall order." Dirk cocked his head slightly. "A bit unrealistic, don't you think?"

This time her gaze shifted to Dylan's and stayed fixed. "I used to."

CHAPTER FIFTEEN

Today was almost an oxymoron, a yin and yang. Both Jo and Dylan and all her family and friends were super excited to see how the first episode turned out, and at the same time, on edge over the blow back it could cause in their personal lives back home.

For Jo, while having her mother think that her youngest daughter was willing to manhunt on live TV would create fodder to be teased for years to come, for Dylan the after effects could be more serious. According to him, the business was doing just fine as is. Even though having this new large account would be a wonderful boom to the firm, losing it wouldn't put them under. Still, the idea of losing it over a stupid effort to help a friend and not over incompetence was the frustrating part.

Though she suspected for Dylan, the bigger part was letting his dad down. That she could certainly understand. Her own father had always been very supportive and never complained or criticized any of his girls. He'd been as enthusiastic about a hand-made paper doll for his birthday when they were little, as a pair of his favorite brand of slacks when his girls were old enough to afford them, but still, it would kill them to truly disappoint their father.

So, now, here they all sat. Even Colleen suffered her way to an upper deck lounge chair to watch the show with the gang. The funniest part of the viewing was that each couple had over the long cruise developed a fan base. Apparently, a very organized fan base. All the passengers seated around Dylan and Jo wore bright blue t-shirts with their names on them. Colin and Debbie's fans were in red t-shirts, and Jay and Sandy's group wore neon pink.

Somehow the bright bubble gum color seemed to suit the younger couple, who Jo was delighted to see, had finally graduated to holding hands *and* smiling at each other. She had a feeling those two—win or lose—had created a solid foundation. Colin and Debbie, well, the words "crash and burn" came to mind. For all their gushing and cooing at the beginning, whatever they had online had not translated well into the real world. At this point, Jo wasn't even sure the pair liked each other, never mind loved.

"Shh," Mina waved at her sisters, "the show is starting."

The rumble of passengers moving about quickly drew to a close. All that could be heard was the sound of the waves lapping against the ship's lower decks and Dirk Simpson introducing the new show from the massive screen.

"You know," Ginnie leaned over, "he's one of Mom's favorite hosts."

Yeah, Jo knew that. She just hoped that Kent's plan to take his future in-laws out to a quiet dinner would be enough to keep her mother out of the loop until her girls were home to put the show in perspective. Of course, that might be easier said than done since even Jo wasn't too sure anymore what that perspective was.

"Oh, no." Teresa laughed. "Do they even know what end of the screwdriver is which?"

Jo had missed the close-up, but was at least thankful it wasn't her or Dylan. For another forty-five minutes, they laughed, gasped, and occasionally cringed at the shots the cameramen had captured. Once she almost cried when the cameras and audio caught Sandy on the verge of a tearful breakdown. In the beginning, the poor kid had been terrified to be on camera.

"Well. That went well." Mina turned to face her family and friends. "All partiality aside, you guys looked good. Really good."

"Yeah." Colleen smiled through an especially pale complexion. "I don't think Dylan and I could have pulled off those looks. I'd have been too busy laughing my butt off."

Mina already had her phone in her hand.

"Checking in with Kent?" Jo asked. Before her sister nodded, she'd realized what a stupid question that was. Who else would she have been in such a hurry to call?

"How'd it go?" Mina asked into the phone. She nodded, muttered uh-huh a few times, and finally with a bright smile gave her sister a thumbs up before standing and walking to the other side of the deck for a little privacy.

"Well, one down. That's a relief." Jo leaned her head back and smiled when Dylan scooted his deck chair closer and took her hand. "Are you going to call your sister?"

He shook his head. "Later. When they're done, she'll update me."

Jo could only hope the results were as good.

"Uh-oh." Ginnie sat up in her chair.

Jo followed suit. "What?"

"Our big sister is marching this way and she looks less than happy."

"Oh, you don't think she had a fight with Kent, do you?" Teresa was now on the edge of her chair.

Mina came to a full stop at the edge of the group's chairs. "We have a problem."

"Kent?" Brenda asked softly.

"I wish." Mina sighed. "While we were talking, Mom asked the bar to change the channel on the overhead TV."

"But the show is over?" Ginnie inched forward as if hearing better would change Mina's answer.

"It is. But they're already advertising next week's show. And guess which sand castle building couple is smiling for the camera?"

All color drained from Jo's face and Dylan wished he could do more than squeeze her hand.

"How'd she take it?" Brenda was the only one in the group brave enough to ask.

Mina's head whipped around to face her maid of honor.

"You tell me. One minute I was talking to Kent about, well, talking to Kent, and all of a sudden I heard an ear piercing scream followed by my mother shouting HUSBAND at the top of her lungs."

"As in, she was in the other room and he couldn't hear her if she didn't yell?" Colleen asked meekly.

Now, Mina turned to her newest friend. "As in the same way she'd scream when my father ate half the cake she'd baked for the church pot luck in an hour."

"Oh." Colleen bit on her lower lips and lifted her gaze to meet Dylan's. She knew as well as he did that this was just the beginning.

Some of the pink had returned to Jo's cheeks. "Then what?"

"I don't know." Mina shook her head and sank heavily into the nearest chair. "Kent muttered *uh-oh*, followed by *No, Mrs. U, it's not what you're* … and the phone died."

"Or got tossed into a pitcher of beer," Ginnie mumbled.

Dylan turned to Jo, and lowering his head, whispered for her ears only, "Would your mother do that?"

Rounded eyes that reminded him of a sweet puppy looking up at you after using your favorite pair of Italian leather shoes as a chew toy, leveled with his just before Jo slowly nodded and sighed. "Oh, she can do worse. We're Italian. We can make a 7.0 earthquake look like a mild upset."

"That bad?"

Her head bobbed again. "I'm afraid so."

Suddenly, waiting for his sister to call him didn't seem like as good an idea as it had only a short while ago.

"I think I'd better go make a phone call of my own."

Jo took her other hand and placed it on top of his, forcing a soft smile for him. "Good luck."

"Thanks."

Making his way clear across the ship, looking over his shoulder every so often to make sure none of the cameramen were behind him, or anywhere near him, he settled into a small corner away from prying eyes. Taking his phone out of his pocket, he took in a deep breath and tapped speed dial for his sister.

The phone rang longer than he thought possible, and just as he expected it to go to voice mail, his sister's breathless voice came on the line. "Hi."

She certainly sounded more chipper than he expected. "Hey. How's it going?"

"Really good. You were right. He loves Eastern European foods."

"Why would I lie?" he said through a stifled chuckle. "Then we're good."

"According to my watch, the show is over and we're safe for now. Mom is setting up the card table. I don't know if it came up in your conversation, but the guy loves to play cards. So we're going to… Mom, what are you doing?"

He didn't like the way her voice rose an octave at that question. "What's wrong?"

"Nothing. Mom is just… Oh, hell."

Before anyone could say another word, the line went dead. He stared up at the starry sky with no idea which one of them had lost the connection or if his sister had just plain hung up on him. There was one thing he knew for sure. Of all the words in the English language, he was learning to very much dislike four of them. *Uh-oh* and *oh hell.*

"Everything, all right?" Jo came up behind him and laid a hand on his forearm.

"That depends."

"On?" She eased around to stand so close he could smell her shampoo. Vanilla.

"If *Oh hell* is better or worse than *uh-oh.*"

CHAPTER SIXTEEN

“Any word yet?” Jo looked at her sister over her morning cup of coffee.

Mina simply shook her head from side to side the same way she'd done every time for the last two days when Jo or Ginnie had.

“How can no one be answering their phones?” Brenda sighed.

“I have news.” Teresa slid into the seat beside the rest of the group. “I decided something has to be wrong besides your mother being madder than a hornet in a cyclone.”

“And?” Ginnie asked.

“Seems the ships public satellite access is down. The ringing we hear is our phones trying to connect. Not the other person refusing to, or unable to, answer.”

Frowns descended on everyone's faces except Teresa.

“Why so glum? That's good news, no?”

“Maybe.” Ginnie took another sip of her morning brew, then swallowed and put the cup back on the saucer. “Or maybe our mother has cut our names out of the family bible and taken all the frozen lasagnas from our freezer.”

“You're equating the importance of the family bible with lasagna?” Brenda stared incredulously at her best friend's sister.

“We're Italian. Food is important to us.” Ginnie shrugged.

Jo gave up any pretense of being hungry and set her fork down on the dish of eggs in front of her. “She won't be mad at you two, she'll be mad at me. Her baby, for not telling her what was going on and for looking for a man on a game show.”

Mina shook her head. "That's where being the oldest gives a person more wisdom. It would be like the old cliché, don't shoot the messenger. We're the messengers, but we'd be crucified, not for delivering the message, but for failing to deliver the message."

As much as Jo hated to admit it, her sister had a point. Tomorrow morning couldn't come fast enough. All she had to do was get through tonight's final tango performance and then in the morning she'd get off this boat and head home to straighten everything out. The only problem being when tomorrow came around, she would be going home without Dylan. She could actually feel little chips of her heart breaking off. The whole mess was the bloody pits.

"Sorry, I'm late. Tried calling my sister and my office. No luck." Dylan slid into the seat next to Jo. The one all her sisters had specifically avoided sitting in.

"Apparently," Jo tipped her head to face him, "the problem is with the ship's public satellite. Calls are neither coming in or going out."

"Oh." He nodded. "I can't decide if that's a good or bad thing."

"Yeah," Jo did her best to smile at him. "That's what I'm wondering."

"On the bright side," Teresa grinned at everyone before continuing, "after tonight this will all be over with."

And that was another part of the problem. As much as she wanted to get home to her mother and the rest of her huge chaotic family, and put this ridiculous game show behind her, deep down, she didn't really want to leave tomorrow. She didn't want this wonderful trip to end.

On a soft sigh, she pushed away from the table and stood to face Dylan. She didn't want to leave him. "Shall we go?"

He bobbed his head, quickly dabbed at the corners of his mouth with the napkin and then setting it down, stood up. "Let's show them how it's done."

His light tone was greatly appreciated at this point of the cruise. The dress rehearsal this morning would be their last chance to practice before the big barbecue bash and final performance at the biggest resort on the island. They had a competition to win, and she very much wanted to.

"See you at the hotel," Mina called after her. The look on her face seemed the most relax since the airing of the TV show and her cut-off conversation with her fiancé. Maybe Teresa's news was a good thing after all.

They'd made it off the ship and caught a cab to take them the short distance to the splashy resort. The lobby was everything a person would expect in the tropics. High ceilings, rattan furnishings, glass end and coffee tables, staff walking about with bright floral shirts, and lots of beautifully colored fresh blooms. The perfect place for the last day of the cruise and the show.

"I'll ask the concierge where the rehearsals are." Dylan's hand was still on the small of her back after ushering her away from the taxi.

"Sounds good."

"Do you want to…" Dylan's mouth froze and his eyes widened. Before she could ask if anything was wrong, he yanked her arm with all his strength and dragged her across the ample lobby and shoved her in a corner behind a potted plant.

"What the…"

His fingers landed on her lips. "Shh." Separating the potted plant like a character in a bad comedy, he narrowed his eyes. "It can't be."

"What can't be?" she whispered, trying to see what he was looking at.

Through the green split leaves, he pointed a finger. "That man over there in the khaki shorts, green shirt, and Panama hat."

It was easy to spot who she was pointing to.

"Either that's Bruce Constantine, or I'm hallucinating."

"Who?" She squinted as if seeing more clearly would enlighten her as to who the heck was Bruce Constantine.

"The owner of Costa Breweries. The big shot we've been trying to win over."

"Why would he be here? I mean, I suppose he has as much right to a vacation as anyone, but here?"

Dylan sighed and then took in a deep breath. "Okay. So what if it's him? This is a big hotel. As soon as he's out of the lobby, we'll find where we need to be and get there as fast as we can."

"Okay." She offered him a wide, reassuring smile and decided that wasn't enough. Still hidden by the massive plant, she stood on her tip toes and kissed him, smack on the lips. Something she'd been wanting to do since that day he'd kissed her almost a week ago.

Curling his arms around her waist, Dylan fell into her kiss. For almost a week, he'd been wanting to do this very thing. Now all he wanted to do was keep her close and kiss her for the rest of the day. To hell with the rehearsal, the show, the money, and thank you to the potted plant for affording them some much wanted privacy. Potted plant. Costa Breweries. Reluctantly, pulling back, he glanced over her shoulder. Constantine was nowhere in sight. "As much as I hate to say this, if we're going to make rehearsal, we need to go now."

On a heavy sigh, Jo nodded, and slipping her hand in his, followed him out from behind the plant. He'd managed to take two, three steps at best, when Jo shoved him back behind the plant. "Oh my heavens."

Somehow, that didn't sound like anything a woman who wanted to make out behind a potted palm would say. Following her gaze, he glanced at several tourists with suitcases walking through the lobby. "What?"

"Maybe we're both hallucinating."

"Constantine?" He looked for the green-shirted man.

Jo shook her head and stuck her finger out halfway through the palm leaves. "My mother."

"What? Are you sure?" He stared at several women, wondering which was the woman the sisters all adored and feared at the same time.

"Yes. I mean no. I mean. Why would she be here? My

mother has left our hometown maybe twice in my lifetime. And that was always in the same state." She blew out a heavy sigh. "Do you think we've both been drugged?"

Shifting her to his side, and sliding his arm around her waist, he shook his head. "Unfortunately, not very likely."

Together they stood stone still watching Mrs. Ummarino cross to the concierge desk and speak to a tall slender brunette with a wide-brimmed straw hat. "Now who is she talking to?"

The two women shifted and Dylan's jaw could have hit the floor. "Maybe we died and went to hell and don't know it." Pointing through the leaves, he raked the fingers of his other hand through his hair. "*That* is my sister."

"And *this* is your father. What are you two doing making yourselves at home with a potted plant?

CHAPTER SEVENTEEN

"**D**ad." Dylan spun around, pulling Jo beside him. "What a surprise."

The tall man with salt and pepper hair, who bore a striking resemblance to his son, lifted his gaze from his confused offspring to the top of the palmed plant and back to Dylan. "I was just thinking the same thing."

"There you all are." The man Jo now knew to be Bruce Constantine stood behind Mr. Barnes.

"Are you having a party without me?" Coming to stand next to the brewery CEO was Jo's very own hallucination.

"Mama?" she managed to mutter.

"Yes." Her mother smiled. *Smiled.*

What the heck was going on? Had she and Dylan somehow stepped into the cab and stepped out in an alternate universe? "Nice to see you?" She hadn't really meant for the greeting to come out like a question, but then again, she wasn't very sure of anything at this very moment.

"May I ask why we're all gathered by this less than stellar botanical garden?" Dylan's sister took one step back, and with a wave of her arm, redirected everyone away from the lone potted plant and out of the corner of the lobby. "Surely there's somewhere more comfortable we can gather?"

Dylan looked at his sister, glanced down at his wrist watch then back up. "We have exactly twenty minutes before we have to be at a dress rehearsal—"

"Ooh," Jo's mom slapped her hands together, "I love dress rehearsals."

"Except no one is allowed at this one, Mama."

"Oh." Her mother's enthusiasm and her smile slipped away.

"As I was saying." Dylan glanced at his watch again. "With only nineteen minutes till we have to be somewhere else, the most comfortable place we have time for is the sofas over there."

All heads nodded and like a mini parade, they marched in single file to the designated spot.

"Who wants to start?" Dylan asked, then raised his hand palm out. "Never mind. I will. Why are my people and Mr. Constantine here?"

"Call me Bruce."

Dylan's brows shot up high before settling back in their proper place. "Okay. Why are you two and—"

"Three," his father said, pointing behind his son. "Your mother's here, too."

"Whatever," Dylan said, as his mother hurried to join the group. "What are you doing at this hotel?"

Dylan's mom spoke up. "We're all here to see the filming of the last episode."

"And how did you know about that?" Dylan stared at his mom.

"Why, from Carson."

Dylan's voice almost cracked. "Carson told you?"

"Well. Not Carson exactly."

"His mother." Dylan sighed.

"I love everything Dirk Simpson has ever done," Bruce Constantine interrupted. "Now I admit, at first I was furious that any lawyer who wanted to represent my company would be off on a frivolous television show. After all, how seriously could such an attorney take his job or my business? But, when I found out that it's a Dirk Simpson show, and then your mother spoke to her friend and got permission to come, I just had to tag along."

"We're all delighted to include you." His father gave Dylan a pointed glare that even Jo knew was a silent message to not rock the boat.

Bruce turned to Dylan's mother. "So nice to finally meet you."

"The pleasure is all mine." Dylan had definitely inherited his mother's high wattage smile.

"Your goulash is delicious." The minute the words were out of Bruce's mouth, Jo felt Dylan stiffen beside her.

"My goulash?" Mrs. Barnes looked down at her dress, brushed at her skirt, and lifted her gaze to the CEO. "I had a sandwich for lunch."

Bruce's brows crumpled in confusion. "No, no. I didn't mean you spilled your goulash, I meant your recipe."

"Recipe?" His mother's eyes rounded as wide as a silver coin. "As in to cook?"

And on that cue, Jo figured it was time to do the famed Ummarino redirect before things got any more messy than they already were. "So," she cleared her throat and turned to her mother. "We know why the Barnes family is here, but why are you here, Mama?"

"Oh, well, of course I was absolutely furious when I realized what was going on behind my back."

"Mama..." She hated that she sounded like a whiney brat.

"We'll discuss you keeping secrets from me later. Now, let me finish answering your question. When Mr. and Mrs. Barnes decided to come see what's happening in person, they asked Carson's mother for your name. Mr. Barnes—"

"Toni, I thought we settled this. It's Robert, not Mr."

What the heck was going on here? Her tough as nails mother smiled and fluttered at Dylan's dad like a kid with a crush on her teacher. Which somehow seemed fitting since no one had called her mother Toni since high school.

"As I was saying," still smiling, her mother faced her again, "Robert here was nice enough to invite your father and me."

"Dad's here too?" Someone just shoot her and take her out of her misery.

"Yes," Jo's mother frowned, "he's having a discussion with the kitchen about their cold cuts. I told him it was none of his business, but you know how your father gets—"

Jo held up her hand. "I get it, Mama." To her father, the proper storage of deli foods was tantamount with maintaining world peace.

"Anyhow, how could I miss my little girl winning the

grand prize for the most in love couple?" The stars in her mother's eyes were as bright as the stars had been in the Caribbean skies.

Just what Jo had so wanted to avoid. Right about now, a fairy godmother would come in really handy. Or better yet, Scotty, beam her up. "About that, Mama. Didn't Mrs. Carson explain this to you?"

Her mother waved her comment off and Jo didn't even know where to begin. The rest of today's show was only going to make it impossible to convince her mother otherwise. Especially if she looked into her daughter's eyes and saw what was really in her heart. Boy, was she ever in trouble with a capital T.

Time was most definitely running out. Their ten days together had gone by too quickly. With a cameraman or microphone around almost all the time, the chaos of the last few days, and now everyone's families showing up on the proverbial doorstep, how was Dylan supposed to straighten anything out between him and Jo? The only place with any real privacy was the toilet—not a very romantic setting.

Nervous and distracted, it had taken him forever to button his fancy white shirt. He knew he was supposed to look like a Latin lover but he felt more like Elmer Fudd in a tux. Unlike the private lessons of before, all three couples were expected to do their routines at the same time in the same place. Exactly the way it would be done on stage in a short while. At least all the men wore the same stupid outfit. Somehow blending in made Dylan feel a little better.

"How do I look?" That soft voice that could melt his heart with a single syllable drifted over his shoulder.

He spun around and almost lost his breath. Only one word came to mind. "Perfect." In a dark red dress that hung lower on one side than the other with a low-cut front and tiny sleeves that barely covered her shoulder, she was more than stunning.

The music began and all three couples took their places. Dylan didn't have to be told to keep his eyes on Jo, he couldn't have torn them away if he tried. From the first few steps, they moved as one, slowly, fluidly, and not once did either of them look away. This was the only thing that had happened all day that felt right.

Holding her close in his arms, her one leg slid back as he lowered her to the ground and then ever so slowly, eased her back up, her torso slithering against his as though they were meant to be one. So very right. How bad would it be if instead of stopping with the music, he continued to hold her and glide across the floor? Keep moving, every step in sync, every sway as one, all the way across the hotel, out the door, and not stopping until they reached a truly isolated spot just for them and no one else.

Eyes still locked on each other, moving so closely together not even a sheet of paper would fit between them, his heart pounded out a rhythm of want, desire, and love that was frightfully new to him.

With a final turn, her back bowed over his arm and her one leg slid forward. Still his eyes remained fixed with hers. The soft white skin of her neck stretched with the tilting of her head, begging to be kissed. But he couldn't, not here, not now.

The last beat of the soulful tango came to an end and he slowly eased her up and into his arms. A round of applause in a rehearsal hall was unexpected. Whether it was for them, the others, or everyone including the instructors, he didn't know, or care. He simply couldn't pretend any longer. Still holding her in the circle of his arms, he dared to blink. "I can't do this."

Jo blinked, a curtain of darkness threatening to dim the bright light in her eyes and he instantly realized his mistake. He'd said too little. She didn't understand.

"I can't pretend this is pretend."

This time when she blinked, confusion filled her gaze.

"I love you, Jo Ummarino. I want all this to be real."

A sweet smile returned to her face. "It is real. I love you, Dylan Barnes."

Applause erupted once again, and despite the woman he

loved in his arms, the outside world slowly crept in. Jo's head nestled perfectly against his shoulder; they turned as one to stare at the side of the room the thunderous applause had come from.

To his surprise, despite the rehearsal not being open to the public, all their friends and family stood in one corner of the room, Carson beside them grinning like a loon.

Jo's mom burst away from the group and sprinting across the wooden floor pulled her daughter out of his arms and into a stuffing squeezing hug. "I knew it," she squealed, then taking a step back, her gaze narrowed, and her hands cupped both sides of Jo's face. "I'm still mad at you for hiding all this." Another smile came over again. "But oh, how happy you look. And you." The woman spun around to face him. "I can see it in your eyes. You love my Giuseppa. Welcome to the family."

Never before had Dylan been hugged so tightly he felt sure that this was what it must feel like to be squished by an Amazonian Boa Constrictor.

"All right, everyone." Carson strode briskly across the ballroom. "We have a show to produce. Only authorized personnel remains." He slowly waved all the friends and family out of the room, then turned back to his friend. "Just so you know, the boom mic picked up most of what you just said. Your family heard every word. But it won't be on the final episode or part of the competition."

"Thank you," they both uttered softly.

Carson nodded. "And by the way, buddy." He waved a finger between them. "I expect your firstborn to be named after me." Laughing, he walked away shouting instructions to different crew members.

"Carson Barnes," Dylan repeated slowly, then turned to Jo, unsure of her reaction. He didn't want to scare her away.

Heaving out a heavy sigh, she turned her gaze from Carson's departing back to Dylan.

At least the sweet smile was still on her face. That had to be a good thing, didn't it?

"I think I like it." Her voice was soft, and low, and flowed over his heart like a sea of warm honey.

Oh, yeah. Definitely a very good thing.

CHAPTER EIGHTEEN

The final competition was upon them and for the first time since starting this crazy charade, Jo didn't care if they won or lost. She didn't even care if they walked away from the whole situation, but neither she nor Dylan could do that to Carson.

Unlike all the previous onboard challenges, the tango competition was not done in one of the lounges, but in the ship's theater. So here she was in the wings, waiting to perform the last event.

"Looks like we made the big time," Dylan teased. Ever since this afternoon's rehearsal, he hadn't let go of her hand. To the rest of the passengers and even their friends, that didn't seem any different than what they'd been doing all along for the sake of appearances, and winning points, but this, this was different. The touch was both lighter and stronger, confident. The warmth—the love—ran from her fingertips to her toes.

She peeked around one of the curtains and could just barely see the guests in the front row. Her family, Dylan's family, and Mr. Constantine were of course, front and center. Even though they'd already seen the performance, having to do this again knowing how carefully her mother would be watching added an extra edge to her nerves. "I didn't realize how big this theater is."

"You'll be wonderful," Dylan leaned in and whispered in her ear. Like earlier, they weren't wearing mics, but she'd learned it didn't matter, production was always listening. Still, the squeeze of his hand over hers, and the warmth of his breath tickling her ear, was enough to almost make her forget their performance would be broadcast all over the ship for a few thousand passengers to watch.

"Just pray I don't trip over my own two feet."

"Not a chance." He smiled at her then lifted her hand and pointed across the backstage area. "More trouble in paradise."

Following the direction he'd pointed, she looked to where Colin and Debbie were doing a last minute practice. "Is he looking at her boobs?"

"I'm afraid so. Should I remind him her eyes are above her shoulders?"

"No need." Jo shook her head. "From the fire in Debbie's eyes and the way her mouth is moving faster than my mom's after we ate the cake she made for the church bake sale, I'd say Debbie's doing a good job of telling him that."

"You know, I almost feel sorry for them."

"I know. They looked so enamored when they arrived on the ship."

"I guess the network and producers were right, bringing the online world into the real world can hold a lot of surprises."

"Good evening, ladies and gentlemen," Dirk's voice filled the massive theater. "We have a surprise for you tonight. We have two special judges joining us, and before the competition begins, they have agreed to do a little dance for you. Of course, it will not be the tango." He paused as if expecting the audience to find the comment funny and then continued. "So please offer a round of applause for the brother and sister dance team from your favorite star studded dance show, Ginger and Geoffrey Howard, performing the Paso Doble."

The thunderous eruption of applause was nearly deafening. The lights dimmed and a spotlight appeared center stage. Slowly, the two siblings appeared from opposite sides of the stage and came together in a breathtaking performance that seemed like a cross between Spanish flamenco and every Latin dance ever invented.

"I've seen them on television. I know they're good." Jo shook her head ever so slightly. "But in person. Wow."

"I was just thinking the same thing. Maybe they should have let them perform last. Now we're all going to look bad."

As far as Jo was concerned, she didn't care if she tripped over her own two feet and landed on her posterior. She'd already won her prize.

Once the two star judges were seating at the podium set up in front of the stage, the three couples took their places.

In complete contrast to Colin and Debbie, who had been staring daggers at each other back stage, Jay and Sandy kept stealing glances, blushing and smiling. At least two of the three couples would go home to a happily ever after, even if Dylan never expected himself to be one of them.

Waiting on stage for the music to begin, Colin and Debbie were all professional. The way she smiled at her partner, no one would ever know she'd been spitting mad only a short while ago. And Colin's transformation from leach to lover, keeping his gaze only on Debbie's eyes was nothing more than miraculous. If nothing else those two should try a career in film, they were natural actors.

The same as they'd done at rehearsal, Dylan pulled Jo close and waited for the familiar tune to start. The difference between then and now was that she was his. As fast as he could after they arrived home, he'd pack up his apartment and move across the state to where Jo lived. Not having ever bought real estate had suddenly made his life easier.

Notes of the traditionally recognized song for a tango filled the room and they slowly, and he hoped gracefully, began to move. Every step felt smoother, lighter, and it took everything in him not to grin at her like a Cheshire Cat. Each move had been flawless. Every step, every swirl, every kick came as easily as breathing. All the couples had moved in and out of first place at different points in the competition, but today they were left in the dark.

No one knew where they stood after last night's ship tallies. The final votes would be up to the television viewers. Carson had explained that viewer voting was key in this type of show, so their positions during the cruise could shift based on later votes once the show aired. The final decisions would come after a two hour finale. The viewers would be allowed to vote for the first hour and the votes would be tallied during the second hour. Not even the production company would know who the winner was until that time.

Still, right now, almost cradling Jo in his arms as they swayed across the wooden floor, he didn't care who won. There was only one prize he cared about, winning Jo's love, and he'd already promised himself he would spend the rest of his life cherishing every minute the two shared together.

The music came to a stop. With a final turn, her back bowed over his arm and her one leg slid forward. The same as it had earlier in the day, the soft white skin of her neck stretched with the tilting of her head, begging to be kissed. Only this time, he didn't hold back, didn't doubt, didn't debate. This time, she was his.

EPILOGUE

"Whoa," Antoinette Ummarino, better known to Ginnie and her sisters, and pretty much anyone who entered the Ummarino home, as Mama, chuckled. Letting go of the wooden spoon, she stopped stirring her famous Sunday gravy and wiping her hands on her apron, turned to her youngest daughter and smacked her hand. "That's for dessert. No nibbling."

Sucking the powdered sugar from her finger, Jo grinned up at their mother. "You know I have a sweet tooth."

From behind her, Dylan wrapped his arms around Jo's waist and lightly kissed her neck. "I'm fond of sweets too."

Jo glanced up at the man she'd been sharing long molten looks with every Sunday night for the last fourteen weeks. Though in reality, she'd probably been sharing those drawn out heated looks more than just Sunday nights.

From where she stood, Ginnie was torn between smiling at how cute Jo and Dylan were, and rolling her eyes at how… well… cute they were. Turning from her spot at the kitchen counter to grab another cucumber for the salad, her gaze fell on older sister. Only Mina and Kent could make slicing tomatoes for the dinner salad look romantic.

So much love bouncing off the walls. It was enough to make Ginnie sigh. At least she wasn't losing her sisters but gaining brothers. Something that came in very handy when things at the house she and her sisters had bought together needed repairing.

"Got here as soon as I could." Colleen, Dylan's long time friend and now a close friend of the entire family, hurried through the front door and glanced at the dishes and trays of food spread across every available surface in the family kitchen. "I just love coming here when I'm hungry."

Mama laughed, and pretty much everyone knew what the woman meant. There was never a shortage of food at the Ummarinos, and everyone was guaranteed to be sent home with a week's worth of leftovers. Something that had been a blessing when after a tough day or week at work, none of the sisters felt like cooking.

Colleen made her way over to where Ginnie had been slicing loaves of Italian bread. "I just love how adorable those two look."

There was no need to ask which two, or to follow the direction Colleen's chin pointed. At any moment in time, a candid shot of Dylan and Jo smiling at each other, silently professing their love with a mere gaze, would make an ideal Valentine's Day commercial. The promise of an adoring mate who looked at the other with the anticipation of an ice cream sundae smothered in whipped cream and cherries, could sell a side of beef to a vegan.

"I don't suppose either of you know who won?" Colleen popped an olive in her mouth and crossed the kitchen to where Jo and Dylan had taken seats side by side in the dining room.

Spoon in hand to dish out her well-loved gravy, her mother whirled around sprinkling red sauce around the kitchen. "I thought we had to wait for tonight's final episode to learn the results?"

Everyone and anyone they'd ever met had arrived at the large family home to spend the afternoon Ummarino family style, and then view the show that would begin in exactly one hour. Each person keenly aware that this would be the only way of learning who would take home the big prize.

Handing off the bread basket to Jo, Dylan shook his head. "Nope. The audience gets one last chance to vote."

Never in all her years had Ginnie seen the family eat so fast and talk so little. And for a loud Italian family like hers, not talking said a whole lot. Except for Jo and Dylan, and Mina and Kent, who continued to do that silent lovey-dovey communicating with only their eyes.

"Why is everyone not in the den?" Their cousin Rosa

stood in the doorway. "The show is starting in two minutes."

Like children following the Pied Piper, dishes and food were left at the table and everyone hurried after Rosa. Large bowls filled with every flavor of popcorn known to man were scattered around the small side tables. Within minutes, everyone was settled in. Of course, Jo and Dylan had curled into each other on the oversized chair designed for one, while Ginnie sat on one of the folding chairs.

Every week for the last thirteen episodes, the heart of the Ummarino family had gathered on Sunday nights to watch the show. The very first clip of contestants' arrival for the cruise showed Jo, tipping her head back, laughing ever so slightly, and laying her hand flat over Dylan's heart. They had to have barely met, and yet, the chemistry was all over the screen. Ginnie couldn't imagine how she'd missed it on the ship. With each episode it would have been obvious to a blind man that the two were falling in love, and yet, it had all blown right over Ginnie's head.

Even now, with Jo's head snuggled into Dylan's shoulder, and their legs casually intertwined, the two didn't just look as though they'd been built for each other, they reminded Ginnie of a single piece of art that had been pulled apart and finally brought back together the way they always were meant to be.

Seated beside Ginnie, the only person in the room whose gaze was not glued to the big screen TV was Colleen. Staring at her phone, one finger repeatedly swiped over who knew what.

"What are you doing?" Ginnie dared to take her eyes off the television, after all, she had been there.

"Just checking my lottery ticket from last night."

Dylan rolled his eyes. "You do realize you've probably spent more money on those tickets since I've known you than you'll ever win. *If* you win."

Flashing him a wide toothy grin, Colleen shrugged. "It's the thrill of the hunt."

A dramatic clip of music played and everyone's attention returned to the TV.

"Oh, don't tell me those two are going to win?" Cousin Rosa frowned at Colin and Debbie. "I don't like them. They're too superficial."

Of the three couples, Ginnie's partiality to her sister aside, she had never taken a liking to Colin and Debbie. Cousin Rosa had nailed the why.

"I like those two," their cousin Toni-Ann pointed at the screen to Jay and Sandy. "They're cute."

Thirty minutes later, the show had been airing what they called *captured moments*. Times when the couples had not realized they were being filmed. The glimpses into the real people had done nothing to push Colin and Debbie up on the scoreboard. Jay and Sandy had managed a few touching moments that made Ginnie smile, but it was the furtive looks and gentle touches between Dylan and Jo that had Ginnie almost losing her breath.

Stealing her gaze away from the TV, she glanced at Jo and Dylan. Had she been clear across the room Ginnie could still have felt the electricity sparking between them, and all they were doing was smiling at each other.

"Oh, no." Rosa frowned and Ginnie looked back to the TV.

Jay and his girl were staring at each other over a flower Jay had picked for her from the side of the road. The way he softly encouraged her, praised her, and just barely rubbed his finger along the base of her thumb, if the audience wasn't rooting for those two before, they would be now. *Blast*.

"Your rehearsal moment was better." Crossing her arms, Mama glared at the television. She was probably right, but Carson had said it would not be aired, and he'd kept that promise.

"And the winner is…"

To Ginnie it looked like every person in the room had inched forward on their chairs. Even Jo and Dylan. They'd both sat up and leaned forward, their hands the only thing still gently intertwined. And finger still poised over the phone, Colleen had let it fall to her lap.

"Jay and Sandy!" the host's voice announced loudly.

"Congratulations!"

A collective groan of disappointment rolled through the room.

Cousin Rosa crossed her arms and leaned back. "We were robbed."

"I never liked that Dirk Simpson." Mama pushed to her feet.

"Holy Moses." Colleen's jaw dropped and her gaze flew to Dylan. "I hit four numbers."

Dylan's head whipped around to face his friend. "What? Let me see that."

His hand outstretched, Colleen handed him her phone. "I can't believe I finally won something."

"Not something." Dylan smiled and handed her back her phone. "Thirty thousand dollars."

Once again Colleen's eyes flew open. "Oh, my, lord. Even after taxes, that's a down payment on a small house or condo." She jumped out of her seat and pumped her fist. "Yes!"

"Not a bad consolation price." Dylan let go of Jo long enough to step forward and give his friend a congratulatory hug.

"Now, that is good news." Mama nodded. "Let's celebrate. I made tiramisu."

The sound of footsteps tapping their way to the kitchen on the hardwood floors echoed all the way down the hall, but no sound came from behind Ginnie. Turning toward the living room, she leaned her head back. "Are you two…"

Standing face to face, Jo's hands cradled in Dylan's much larger ones, their gazes locked on each other like heat lasers. Ginnie couldn't have turned away if she wanted to.

"I had a long talk with Cassie and Dad this morning. We all agreed, no matter the outcome of the show tonight, Cassie is all the partner the firm needs. I'm not going back to the firm. I'm going to do what I've dreamed of for a long time. Start my own custom furniture business. Handcrafted, like so many years ago."

"I can help you with your marketing. I'm pretty good at it."

"I know, but I've already got my first order for a complete dining room suite."

"Oh, that's wonderful!"

"Life has an interesting sense of humor. It's Bruce."

"Constantine?"

Dylan nodded.

"Guess he'll be a client of yours after all. You're already on your way to having everything you've wanted."

"Not quite." He reached into his pocket and Ginnie had to cover her mouth to stop from gasping out loud. A black velvet box appeared in the palm of his hand. "If you'll agree to marry me, then I'll have everything I've ever wanted."

Lips pressed tightly together, Jo bobbed her head up and down without stopping as Dylan slipped the ring onto her finger. For a short moment she stared at the diamond shining up at her before throwing her arms around his neck and giving him a long hard kiss that Ginnie had no business watching.

Turning away, she took two steps when her cousin Rosa yelled from the kitchen. "Are you growing roots in the hall? Dessert is almost gone. My brother is coming in for thirds."

"Coming." Ginnie blew out a sigh and stared down the hall. Two sisters, two cruises, and two men too good to be true. What were the odds of that happening? Shaking her head, she knew the answer. She was so very happy for both her sisters, but she couldn't help feeling she was being left behind. Or worse, that she might never catch up. Maybe she'd have better luck with the lottery. Moving toward the kitchen, she nodded. Tomorrow, she'd buy a ticket.

MEET CHRIS

USA TODAY Bestselling Author of dozens of contemporary novels, including the award winning Aloha Series, Chris Keniston lives in suburban Dallas with her husband, two human children, and two canine children. Though she loves her puppies equally, she admits being especially attached to her German Shepherd rescue. After all, even dogs deserve a happily ever after.

More on Chris and all her books can be found at
www.chriskeniston.com

Follow Chris' Monday Blog at her website
ChrisKenistonAuthor

Follow Chris on Facebook at
ChrisKenistonAuthor

Never miss a New Release! Sign up for News from Chris:
www.chriskeniston.com/newsletter.html

Questions? Comments?
I would love to hear from you! You can reach me at:
chris@chriskeniston.com

9 798891 490000